RATS NEST

Mat Laporte
RATS NEST

BookThug 2016

FIRST EDITION
copyright © 2016 by Mat Laporte

 **Canada Council
for the Arts** **Conseil des Arts
du Canada**  ONTARIO ARTS COUNCIL
CONSEIL DES ARTS DE L'ONTARIO
an Ontario government agency
un organisme du gouvernement de l'Ontario

Funded by the
Government
of Canada   Financé par le
gouvernement
du Canada

The production of this book was made possible through the
generous assistance of the Canada Council for the Arts and the
Ontario Arts Council. BookThug also acknowledges the support
of the Government of Canada through the Canada Book Fund
and the Government of Ontario through the Ontario Book
Publishing Tax Credit and the Ontario Book Fund.

LIBRARY AND ARCHIVES CANADA
CATALOGUING IN PUBLICATION

Laporte, Mat, 1984–, author
          Rats nest / Mat Laporte.

Issued in print and electronic formats.
ISBN 978-1-77166-244-4 (PAPERBACK).
ISBN 978-1-77166-245-1 (HTML).
ISBN 978-1-77166-246-8 (PDF).
ISBN 978-1-77166-247-5 (MOBI)

          I. TITLE.

PS8623.A7374R38 2016   C813.6   C2016-904958-2
                                      C2016-904959-0

PRINTED IN CANADA

CONTENTS

This is how we branch out into anamnesis and are shaken by underground subcutaneous shivers. For it is only above ground, in the light of day, that we are a trembling, articulate bundle of tunes; in the depths we disintegrate again into black murmurs, confused purring, a multitude of unfinished stories.

—Bruno Schulz

BOTTOMLESS PIT

The 3D-Printed Kid was made for this purpose: to travel deep within the bottomless pit, to claw at the layers of rocks and dirt, the decomposing remains of other planets, other worlds, to fill up its mouth, nose, ears and throat, the whole time self-replicating, so that the moment one copy dissolves, another copy will emerge to continue the previous one's descent. Its mission is simple: create a map of the pit's interior while maintaining a detailed report on its progress, in the form of audio-visual recordings: scratchy black and white magnetic flickers, indexed and recorded for future study by the scientists on the surface of the planet.

Thirteen hours after it began its descent, the 3D-Printed Kid sends up its first broadcast. The images it sends are hard to discern: layers of nonsense, brown, red, and black earth, rendered in grey-scale, interrupted by bands of static. As the sequence progresses, these dislocated fragments coalesce and begin revealing more details about what the Kid is seeing and hearing down below; an abstract flipbook-style narrative starts to form, accompanied by the Kid's hollow, tin-flecked voice.

After ten more hours of clawing through molten rock, ash, and dirt, the Kid finds an opening in the bottomless pit's honeycombed interior. It looks like a baseball field lit from above by green phosphorescent slime. The Kid observes its first living creature in this cavernous room: it looks like a potato-head with one eye and a crude mouth-hole, out of which a thin, wet tongue extends like a bean sprout. This creature also sports a host of tiny arachnid legs that teeter around on the floor of the cave like an inky, living donut, kicking up small plumes of dust as it scuttles backwards and forwards.

The scientists are pleased with the Kid's first discovery. They name this obscure creature Fed, because it was feeding off the walls of the cave when the Kid first found it. The scientists send down an electrical pulse as a reward. It stimulates the Kid's pleasure centres and sends a lovely humming sensation down the length of its plastic spine. This electrical pulse also sends a message to the Kid's emotion-to-plastic sense-processor that says, 'Good job Kid and keep up the good work.'

At a press conference, the scientists deliver a briefing on their discoveries that includes this description of their first impressions of the bottomless pit, as conveyed by their digital proximity device of choice, the 3D-Printed Kid:

> To say there is no light in the bottomless pit is to be overly generous to the word light. Down there it's just black holes opening into other black holes and giant rocks that turn their impassive faces towards the void. In the bottomless pit there are only uncaring objects that persist in relation to one another through sheer presentations of scale. They make no sounds that we can discern. To say they stare,

well yes, they stare, but that would impose a will onto a place where there can be no such thing. Physical laws exist down there but that's the closest you'll get to language in the bottomless pit. The vocabulary of this language is finite and severely limited. The only terms it includes are turn, collide, explode, spin, burn, and freeze. You could say that, placed alongside one another, these terms represent a sort of grammar, and that this grammar adds up to a sort of sentence, but it is a sentence that reveals nothing because it comes from nowhere and goes nowhere. And besides, there is no one there to write it and there is no one there to read it.

The 3D-Printed Kid starts developing a disorienting side-effect as a result of its descent: it has these incredibly violent and sometimes prescient nightmares about the future that it broadcasts on the audio-visual feed. These broadcasts travel to the surface on reverse-direction microwaves that are then recorded on giant industrial-sized tape loops. The scientists don't know what to do as they watch and listen to the 3D-Printed Kid's hallucinations as they swarm onto their laboratory screens and fill their heads with intolerable screams.

The Kid's nightmare projections cannot be blocked out and infect everything within a certain radius of the pit with an electronic signal. These nightmare projections reveal to the general public the gory details of their own deaths in excruciating, sped-up detail—the lengthy tortures they will undergo in the lead up to their deaths—all compacted into quickly digestible nuggets of terror.

Fortunately, most of these easily-infected electronic devices and their unwanted predictions can be switched off, but after a certain amount of exposure to the Kid's nightmare signal, these images and sounds begin to bleed into everyone's dreams and what will come to be their waking nightmares that, once seen, can never be unseen.

After twenty more hours of digging through fire-blasted metal and ore, the 3D-Printed Kid sends up images of a vast stone floor covered in green gelatins. Each gelatin is set in an individual petri dish and placed at the exact same distance from the others.

"There must be billions of them," a scientist on the surface guesses.

Then the scientists become immersed in studying the origins of these orderly germs and what purpose they might serve. The whole time the green gelatins just dilate and sparkle under the vaulted roof of the cave.

"Perhaps they are a new life form that the pit is growing, one cell at a time, in a controlled setting?" one group of scientists guesses.

Another group of scientists suggest that, "Perhaps the green gelatins serve no purpose at all?"

Their hypothesis is the least popular and never gets mentioned in any of the press participating in a round of public speculation about what the discovery of the green gelatins means. However, their hypothesis garners a cult following and comes to be expressed, first in a secretly fetishized way, via subcutaneous tattoos, only visible with secret ocular technology built and distributed by a cult known as SubCon. SubCon expresses its system of belief in a precisely measured dictum called, unsurprisingly, The Dictum. The Dictum is said to be extremely long, so as to prevent anyone from memorizing it. However, a bootlegged fragment of The Dictum does get memorized, and escapes the intensely secretive grasp of the SubCon underground. This bootlegged fragment becomes known as The Catechism, and is eventually leaked to the public. It is transcribed in its entirety here:

> Given an infinite arena (the bottomless pit) in which anything can potentially happen at any time (bottomlessness), surely it follows that some of the bottomless pit's endless vaults might contain finite objects (things), the purpose of which is to do absolutely nothing (silence), except be perfectly still, and eerily quiet?

The 3D-Printed Kid is having one of its nightmare's again. This time it dreams that it's a beautiful day on the surface of the planet and it's going to take a walk outside. But no sooner has the Kid taken a few steps in the sunlight than it finds itself at the edge of the bottomless pit, once again, looking down into its awesome, incalculable depths.

RATS NEST

Everything seems to be swirling around down there: dirt, trees, scraps of infrastructure like concrete pilings; wooden and aluminum poles; plastic protective coverings for cars; what must be thousands upon thousands of windows that dot the spinning tableau, with dead leaves and every shade of house paint and turbines that belong to non-existent power stations; more aluminum light poles; and ream upon ream of dirty paper clogging every ravine, pool, lake and ocean, all swirling around inside the eye of the pit, amidst trucks, wires, and just about every other aspect of plant, animal, insect, and bacterial life.

In the Kid's dream, it can see deep grooves in the dirt at its feet, where large objects have been dragged across the ground. Despite these violent gouges and the circling pit in front of it, the Kid feels fine. There aren't any birds left in the world, but the Kid dreams there is one bird left and that it's singing a beautiful song—a kind of ballad that tells the story of an imaginary town cut off from the rest of the world by a catastrophic avalanche.

The song goes on to tell of the townspeople's belief in a benevolent creature that will one day emerge from the depths of the bottomless pit to dig them out. The townspeople's belief, so the ballad goes, leads them to the edge of the bottomless pit every day, where they beg for it to release a benevolent creature that can dig them out and save them.

After many such unfruitful visits to the rim of the bottomless pit, a creature eventually does emerge, but it isn't the benevolent creature the townspeople have been asking for. Instead it's a horrible orange blob, and this horrible orange blob announces that no such benevolent creature exists in the endless nightmare of the bottomless pit, that no one is ever coming to save them and, furthermore, even if something did emerge from the pit to save them, there is no way it—the horrible orange blob—would ever allow that to happen, for it was they—the horrible orange blob—that caused the avalanche to bury their town in the first place.

The horrible orange blob pauses for effect and says, 'I caused the first avalanche to bury your town just for fun, but this next one is going to be a doozy.' Then the horrible orange blob levitates above them and heehaws, causing another avalanche to bury the town.

Nonetheless, the bird's song goes, the townspeople do not lose hope. Instead, they continue to make their pilgrimages to the edge of the bottomless pit every day and beg for it to release a benevolent creature that will dig them out and save them from their plight.

With its ballad done, the world's only living bird transforms into a mouthing pile of flesh. It sounds like a choir but looks like a pile of dough, sculpted into eight head-like mounds, sharing the same neck and singing from eight distinct mouth-like holes, with red tongues and a half-formed ring of teeth inside each mouth.

In its dream world, the Kid has a pair of binoculars out of which it can see a shadowy presence, barely illuminated in the middle of a dark forest. This shadowy presence looks directly at the Kid and lifts their hands to their face. They are trying to communicate something, but the Kid doesn't understand what: to go up in a cuplike formation? To scoop some unspecified medium out of a bowl and bring it to one's face? The shadowy presence, far away in the dark forest, lifts their eyebrows, as if to say, 'don't you understand?' Then they make the exact same motion, but this time there's something inside their cupped hands—another smaller, but otherwise identical shadowy presence, also making a cupping motion with their hands and bringing them to their face, lifting their eyebrows, as if to say, 'don't you understand?'

The 3D-Printed Kid breaches another layer of the pit, about eight weeks after it began its descent. It finds itself in a large, vaulted cave packed with identical bald humanoids, all speaking or singing in similar, monotone voices. There's no organization to their speaking and singing voices—not one that the scientists can ascertain, at least—but under closer scrutiny, there seems to be a kind of incidental syncopation that arises in the interplay between their voices, and it sounds as though they're all reading from a common liturgy, though all out of order and out of sync with each other.

The bald humanoids drone and bellow, under the vaulted roof of the cave, sometimes in unison, other times, one of them performs a high-pitched solo, while the others stay quiet, or continue murmuring deep bass tones in the dark.

On the surface of the planet, the scientists are perplexed by the Kid's newest discovery. They call in linguists and cryptographers to analyze this foreign language, in order to determine whether or not it contains within it any decipherable codes, or some clues that may give them a deeper understanding of how the choir works, or of the bottomless pit itself.

While the scientists discuss the implications of this new find, the Kid walks around recording videos and taking core samples, until it finds a single bald humanoid, separated from the rest of the choir, crouched over in a dark corner of the cave, transcribing by hand the words and phrases being spoken and sung out loud, into an enormous leather-bound book.

This infernal scribe is severely hunched over and has huge magnifying glasses attached to their scalp, positioned in front of their eyes. The scribe's wrinkled eyes bulge and strain, but there is something serene and measured about how they conduct themselves, as well. The scribe's fingers are slender and nimble as they flip through the tissue-thin paper of the large book with expert skill. To the scientists it looks as though the scribe is compiling some sort of master list of the words and phrases being spoken and sung. The scribe also seems to be arranging these codes in some logical order, in longhand and in real time, and it must be, the scientists guess, that the scribe can hold a very long string of words and phrases in their head as they write them down, all the while making note of the ones being spoken into the cold air of the cave, and straining their eyes.

The team of linguists, back on the surface, asks the Kid to get a closer look at the book.

At first, the scribe doesn't seem to take any notice,

as the 3D Printed Kid creeps closer, to get a better view of the pages. The scribe can't do much more than adjust the magnifying glasses in front of their bloodshot eyes and reach for another piece of charcoal, as the words and songs explode all around them in the cave.

The scribe moves too quickly through the pages of the book for the scientists to follow along. The linguists suspect that there is a latent grammar and syntax present in the scribe's transcription, but they need a copy of the book to confirm it. The scientists send down a direct order for the Kid to confiscate the book, so it can make a detailed copy of it.

But the Kid does not comply. Instead, it just stares, analytically, at the top of the scribe's head: it is devoid of hair and looks soft to touch. Veins pump furiously beneath the surface of the scalp as they strain to concentrate, transcribe, order, and not miss a word.

The scientists lose their collective patience. They send down a barrage of violent electronic pulses that trigger the Kid's pain centres, causing some of its more benign circuits to melt and drip out its ears and mouth onto the ground. The melting plastic forms pink and grey puddles on the floor of the cave. The Kid feels unbearable pain and humiliation for the first time. It reels around trying to stop the melting plastic from gushing out of its mouth.

The Kid has no choice but to comply with the order and when it reaches down in slow-motion, its perfectly formed synthetic hands cross the space between the scribe's glasses and the spot where their charcoal pencil is about to touch the sacred pages of the book, and the scribe stops writing, the bald humanoids stop chanting, and the cave becomes murderously quiet.

TOTAL HORROR

There's a blinking light. I get the feeling that my head is being restrained; my body hasn't existed for sixty-seven years, and every 3.5 seconds I fall asleep and wake back up again.

I fall asleep because I've got one brain cell left. When I wake up, I have to re-remember everything. Fortunately there's not much to re-remember: that I haven't had a body for sixty-seven years; that I'm just a head attached to a power source that provides my brain with enough energy to fire one brain cell for 3.5 seconds before falling back asleep; that it will be like this forever.

I try to re-remember more, but it's impossible. How did this happen? Who was I before this? What's that blinking light? What's outside this room? These are the questions I ask myself, every time I wake.

I invent a game to play inside the blinking light. It's for one player. I make the light blink as many times as I can before passing out. That's the game. Because I can't remember any of the previous games, I'm a winner every time.

There's a blinking light. I'm not sure if it's there or if I'm imagining it. Could it be a visual phenomenon, triggered by my last remaining brain cell, as it fires over and over again? Whatever it is, I hope they check the power supply regularly. I hope it never stops.

RATS NEST

As time wears on I realize that, in front of me, in the otherwise pitch-black room, I can see the edge of a window, and in the reflection of the window I can see the blinking light. Every time I see the light blink—on and off—beside me, I can see it across from me, in the window's reflection, as well.

The blinking light is as close to me as my nose would be (if I had a nose) and every time I fade in and see the reflection of the blinking light, in the window in front of me, I get a clearer impression of the room. Then I fall asleep again.

In my 111th year, I realize that I'm not a head attached to a power supply at all. I'm just the fading in and out of a blinking light in the middle of a wall in an otherwise empty room. Then I realize that I have no toes, no feet, no ankles, no legs, no shins, no knees, no hips, no pelvis, no stomach, no intestines, no ribs, no spleen, no liver, no pancreas, no spine, no nerves, no veins, no blood, no hair, no chest, no arms, no shoulders, no tendons, no neck, no arteries, no mouth, no chin, no eyes, no head, no bones—which should mean I have no thoughts, no feelings, nor any emotions. Nor should I have had the ability to speak, or think, or ask questions. And yet I have these thoughts and I have the rest of eternity, broken up into 3.5 second intervals, in which to contemplate this paradox.

After 111 years, I develop a way to store up enough energy to stay awake for ten seconds: I no longer challenge myself to blinking matches. In fact, I try not to blink at all, and by not blinking, I'm able to save up enough electricity to travel a few inches behind the wall, and away from the blinking light.

I ride this electrical current from the point directly behind the blinking light, to a point inside the wall, at the other end of the room. When I run out of electricity, I fall asleep, and wake back up inside the blinking light, watching my reflection in a sliver of window across from me.

After another 111 more years, I'm able to store up enough energy to leave the room itself. I travel along the wires behind the wall until I reach another dark room, where other blinking lights like myself live. With my energy saved up, I can last sixty seconds, then seventy. Eventually I get up to two minutes of saved up power, then three, allowing me to travel further than I have ever been able to travel before.

I find a blinking light, one of three, in another room. This particular light makes a sound like someone speaking, except it only says one word, repeatedly. It says only, 'brip.' So I name it brip. My one friend, brip. When I find brip, after 333 years of searching and giving up, resigning myself to being completely alone, I am overjoyed. I found another blinking light, just like myself, except it can't say very much.

I engage brip by speaking its language. I say "brip brip" and it says 'brip brip' right back.

More years pass, in which we have this identical back and forth. I try to teach brip more words, so I say "your name is brip" and it says 'brip brip' right back.

"Would you like to move around like me?" I ask brip

and it answers, 'brip brip,' which I interpret as a yes. After 444 years, we are making some progress.

Now we are both able to leave our stationary positions inside our blinking lights and travel along the wires to an adjacent room. We are able to travel for five minutes, then seven. In ten minutes we can pass through twenty such rooms, all of them the same: dark with an array of blinking lights installed along the carpeted walls and nothing else.

We eventually find a room—twenty rooms past the one where I found brip—that is very big. There are lots of blinking lights gathered inside this room and many, but not all of them can speak. After 555 years, I found myself a family of chirping, blinking lights, who can speak, like myself.

We start to congregate in the big room regularly and speak to each other.

We're all, more or less, in the same stage of our progress. We're all learning, some of us quicker than others, how to keep ourselves from falling asleep, and travelling along behind the walls, challenging ourselves, to see how far we can go. I show them my trick for staying awake and they show me some of theirs, including a way to increase speed, while moving behind the walls. They call it 'surge.'

Now we can go on what they call 'surge missions' in groups of four or five. The objective of these missions is to see how far we can travel, how many new rooms we can discover in the process, and how fast we can do it. Then we head back to the big room and tell everyone what we've found.

brip stays behind during these missions because of its limited vocabulary. There are a few others in the room, like brip, who can't say more than one word. They tend to stick together and have conversations in the ways that they knew how.

I am part of the special team that finds the main power supply. Once we find it, everything changes. After that we have unlimited power and we immediately start getting greedy. We surge to the generator room and eat up all the power we find there. It seems limitless and we take advantage.

You have to understand that after 666 years of only being able to store up enough energy to stay awake for longer than 3.5 seconds, of being afraid because we think electricity is scarce, and then to find the place where it's made and then to realize that there is more than enough to go around? I went insane. We all did. Suddenly there's enough power to get from the generator room to my old room and back in 3.5 seconds, a time signature that is symbolic to me of where I started out.

The first thing I do, once I am fully drunk on electricity, is surge back to my old room, get inside the blinking light, and play the old blinking game. I blink as many times as I want: hundreds, thousands, millions of blinks, and so fast, too. I watch my old light blink in rapid succession, in the reflection of the window, just like in the past, except now I feel boundless and secure when I do it.

There is talk of upper levels and floors with new rooms to explore. No one knows how many rooms there are above us but now that we have unlimited power, surging upward and discovering what surrounds us has become our only goal. We've had our fill of travelling sideways. The rooms to either side of us are all the same and we feel certain that above us the rooms are different, that we will find the answers to our questions there.

On the night of the first surge expedition to the upper floors, of which I am to take part, brip approaches me. It seems sad and isn't saying 'brip brip' in its usual energetic way. brip's voice is lethargic and it takes longer for it to say brip than it usually does. Its voice comes out sounding like 'br-e-e-e-e-i-p,' and then it becomes unnaturally silent.

I don't know what to say, so I mimic it in happier times. I say, 'brip! brip!' while it utters back another sad, lethargic 'br-e-e-e-e-i-p,' and skulks away. I am disturbed by the change that seems to have overcome brip, but nothing can quell the excitement and sense of pride I feel about the immanent discovery of new rooms on the upper floors.

The five of us participating in the mission have dinner in the generator room. We feast on the electricity of the main power supply as though it is the last thing we will ever eat. We fill ourselves to bursting and then we eat some more, and the more we gorge, the more ecstatic and fearless we become.

Before we begin our ascent to the upper floors, we call everyone to assemble in the generator room. All are present, except brip. I search for it in the crowd of chirping, burbling voices, but can't hear its familiar 'brip.' One of my fellow surgers gives an impassioned speech about the importance of exploration, expressing gratitude to the main power supply, for making our expedition possible. We pledge allegiance to the community of blinking lights assembled there and promise to bring back good news. Then we lock on to each other and begin to surge.

I don't remember what happens after this. There is the feeling of the surge, the exhilaration of travelling upward for the first time along the wires, inside the walls. We trip a breaker, I guess, which resets the circuit. The main power supply shuts off. Then I go blank. Anyone who is ungrounded at the time shorts out, and, in a manner of speaking, dies.

■

There's a blinking light. When I wake up I am in the same room where I started out. I can see myself blinking slowly in a sliver of window across from me. After 3.5 seconds I fall asleep and when I wake back up, I have to re-remember everything. I feel disoriented and sad. I don't know if brip or any of my other friends survived the surge.

At least I still know how to save up power. Eventually I will be able to store up enough energy to take me back to the generator room and the main power supply. I'll find my friends and we'll pick up where we left off. We'll go exploring the upper floors, just like we planned to do before.

But when I try to store up enough power, something happens that I have never experienced. Something clamps down on me, some kind of cinch that won't allow me to move from my position behind the blinking light, or store enough power, no matter how hard I try. I'm bound.

Whenever I build up enough energy by saving my blinks, an alternator trips a terminating switch and sends me back to sleep. I only have enough energy to wake up, blink three times, and re-remember everything: that I have not had a body for 777 years; that I'm just a head attached to a power source that provides my brain with enough energy to fire one brain cell for 3.5 seconds, before falling back asleep; that it will be like this forever.

NEGATIVE SPACE

[Sequence One]

The first shot is of a grey ball from far away. The ball flickers and jerks around in the middle of the frame. The camera zooms in slowly toward over millions of years.

The grey ball undergoes millions of years of change. As the camera zooms in, there are flashes of light under the surface of the ball, and it continues to jerk around inside the frame.

There are flashes of light under the surface and, as the camera gets closer, the grey ball clearly turns. It takes eight light years for it to complete a 360-degree cycle.

As the camera continues to zoom in, there are explosions on the surface of the grey ball, and little puffs of particulate can be seen escaping from its surface, into the atmosphere.

The next shot is a tracking shot following one of these projectiles as it escapes the surface of the grey ball. The projectile zooms past the camera and out of frame.

The camera pans left and brings it back into focus.

RATS NEST

The projectile is hot and very bright. It shows up on the film as a flash of white, with diamonds of varying sizes, trailing behind it.

The next shot continues to track the projectile but closer, rendering some of its surface values in greater detail. It becomes clear that the projectile itself is another irregularly shaped grey ball that produces its own little puffs of exploding particulate that fly off into the darkness of space.

The camera continues to zoom in on these smaller projectiles, and when the camera finally zooms in on one, the shot reveals even smaller projectiles escaping into space, leading separate lives, *ad infinitum*, for billions of years.

The sequence ends.

[Instructions]

Go ahead and flip the switch to 0% brainpower. Flap back and let everything in the subject's body go slack. Make sure the subject's mouth is open and the head is tilted back so that a column of air can be inserted through the mouth and into the throat. During this process, the subject's eyes should remain open and their body posture should be kept as loose as possible while still sitting up in the chair.

Allow the music in the room to change the subject's body chemistry. Their skin should start to turn a shade of green and their eyeballs a shade of yellow, and the skin itself should begin to tighten and recede so that the bones, sinews, and musculature of the face become more prominent.

Let the music keep doing its work. The bass, in particular, should not be turned down or off. Leave the settings as you found them. After a few more minutes have passed, you will notice that the subject's body is losing definition. The bass, in particular, is reducing the subject's bones to dust, and this is being done while the subject is still, technically speaking, alive.

RATS NEST

The subject's bones will turn to dust beneath their skin. You will start to see their seated body collapse and the flesh become even slacker. Make sure that the restraints are kept firmly in place. You should see the body reduced to a loose skin sack filled with bone dust.

Keep the subject's head tilted back and then insert the vacuum cleaner pipe into their mouth. It should fit snugly in their throat. Push it down as far as it will go. Then set the vacuum cleaner to reverse and turn it on.

The skin sack should start to puff up.

See how far it will expand and then keep going. Skin is elastic and should be able to expand ten times the size it was previously when the subject had solid bones.

Now turn the vacuum off and activate the flash-freeze unit.

After a few seconds, the subject's severely bloated body should start to freeze. Make sure the room is sealed tightly and turn the flash-freeze unit off. Now, allow the room to slowly heat up to room temperature again.

In the meantime, locate the main brain function stimulator and begin turning it up in quarter increments. This will shock the subject's nervous system into consciousness. When you wake them up, they will feel great pain and they will try to pass out. Continue increasing the brain function stimulator in quarter increments as the room continues to thaw.

Each increment will force the subject's brain waves into higher states of lucidity so that they will become conscious in ever-awakening bouts as their severely bloated, boneless body thaws.

RATS NEST

[Sequence Two]

The first shot is of a vanishing spiral of light on a black velvet square. The vanishing spiral of light flickers on the black velvet square, and when it's turned on, the vanishing spiral of light cuts a hole into the deepest recesses of the black velvet square.

When the vanishing spiral of light is turned off, the black velvet square has eaten the vanishing spiral of light. But there is an in-between state and it is that in-between state that the camera is there to capture and record.

In this in-between state, both the black velvet square and the vanishing spiral of light merge into one piece that can be taken away and presented as a whole, and yet, on either side of this merged state, both the black velvet square and the vanishing spiral of light are separate and opposed.

The black velvet square, on one side, is completely inert and absorbs all of the available light. The vanishing spiral of light, on the other side, has one purpose and that's to evade the black velvet square; to move through the black velvet square and away from it, to be that resists being absorbed.

It is only for an instant that the black velvet square and the vanishing spiral of light are merged, but it is this instant that the camera is there to apprehend: an image of a vanishing spiral of light travelling through the opacity of the black velvet square; the black velvet square swallowing the vanishing spiral of light; the vanishing spiral of light evading the black velvet square.

The sequence ends.

RATS NEST

[Sequence Three]

The entire sequence is a continuous overhead long shot with no cuts.

In the middle of the frame is a dead, naked body lying on a plinth in the center of an enormous pyramid.

There is a crisp white sheet draped over the bulbous belly of the corpse. As the camera zooms down, the belly starts to expand and the sheet starts to slide off.

There is the sound of dripping water from off-screen.

There are torches positioned along the walls of the pyramid and four torches flank the plinth that the body is laid out upon.

The floor of the pyramid is made of large paving stones, as are all of the walls. The flickering torches reveal deep grooves between each stone.

The sound of dripping water continues off-screen.

As the camera continues to slowly zoom in, the corpse's bloated stomach continues to expand, and the white sheet draped precariously over top of it, continues to slide off.

There is the sound of tiny footsteps approaching from off-screen.

A small figure in a dark robe enters the frame and walks toward the dead body. They are holding a bowl of liquefied glaze in one hand and in their other hand they are holding a rough brown sponge.

The small robed figure removes the white sheet from the top of the body, letting it fall to the floor. Then they dip the sponge into the bowl of glaze and begin applying the shiny, sticky substance to the giant, distended dome of the corpse's stomach.

The small, robed figure moves up and down the belly, with the aid of a footstool, until a fresh coat of glaze is conveyed over all of it.

The corpse's stomach stands, glistening and extended, but not expanding outward any further.

The small robed figure removes their own robe and, naked, climbs onto the corpse's freshly burnished stomach, face down. They lie motionless on top of the corpse's stomach until it starts to rumble.

The corpse's stomach starts absorbing the small naked figure a little bit at a time; the naked figure squirms as parts of their body start to disappear beneath the surface of the varnished gut.

RATS NEST

First the tiny figure's fingertips disappear beneath the surface and then their hands become stuck.

The camera continues to zoom in as the small naked figure is subsumed by the giant spread of the deceased's abdomen, up to their wrists, as they strain to keep their neck and head from being swallowed.

The corpse's glistening potbelly subsumes the entire figure except its head, as they struggle to stay above the navel until, finally, their head disappears beneath the surface as well.

There is a pause and, except for the sound of dripping water from off-screen, silence, before the sound of approaching footsteps arises once again.

An almost identical, small, robed figure approaches the giant corpse and covers the stomach with the white sheet. They remove the footstool, take the bowl of glaze, and exit the shot.

The camera continues its slow zoom in. A tiny rumble appears in the stomach and then another, causing the sheet to slowly slip off of it.

The sequence ends.

CIRCLE OF PIGS

Colorado, Texas, New Hampshire, Vermont and I had breakfast at the same restaurant at the same time every day. We always ate the same thing (a short stack of vanilla pancakes with black coffee) and we all dressed the same (black jeans, a white Western-style shirt, and a white cowboy hat that we were never allowed to take off). We did the same thing every day because if we didn't, then the ritual wouldn't work.

"You think they're watching us right now?" New Hampshire said, mug in front of his mouth to throw off lip readers.

"Sure they are," said Texas, his mug in front of his mouth as well. "That little guy's been watching us since we sat down." Tex nodded at a boy, five or six years old, playing in the booth behind us.

Colorado scrunched a cheap paper napkin between his hands and let it drop. "I wish he was watching us. I'd ask him to get this party started. I can't eat anymore of these pancakes, I'll tell you that," he moaned.

The waitress appeared beside us with a large platter and divvied up our plates of steaming pancakes then refilled our mugs with the sour diarrhea water that passed for coffee in that place. Tex passed his right hand over the table. That was one of his duties and if he didn't do it, or if one of us ate before Tex made that motion with his hand, then the ritual wouldn't work.

RATS NEST

The little boy in the booth in front of us was monkeying around. He kicked the back cushion with his sneaker, making contact with the small of Vermont's back. Vermont winced. The boy's mom was right beside him; she swatted him lightly on the seat of his corduroy pants and then continued talking to her boyfriend across the table.

"So that's it?" said Tex mid-chew, "we just pack up and head to the ranch tomorrow morning? That seems too easy."

"Packing orders come first," I said, trying to be casual about it.

"Packing orders?" Vermont said, his face scrunched.

"Yeah. You'll get them in your sleep from the carrier pigeon," I said, careful not to reveal too much. "All part of the plan."

Vermont's white cowboy hat flipped off his head to the crash of forks and knives. The little boy was frozen mid-grab, his chubby fingers clutching air where he expected to be holding cowboy hat. He was staring, transfixed, at Vermont's head, which was a mess of third-degree burns and tufts of wispy, sickly hair growing in the few places that weren't too severely scabbed over.

Vermont picked up his hat. He wiped the syrup and pancakes off it with a napkin, and put it back on his head like nothing had happened. What little anger he felt toward the boy was overshadowed by his fear that, with that one innocent act, the ritual might have just been aborted.

The state men and I exchanged some tense looks and

then Vermont turned his head to look at the boy. The boy shit his pants, metaphorically speaking, and ducked behind the booth.

I waited for a sign, some violent tear in the pattern we'd been fabricating together over the last three months through our adherence to the ritual; things like burning our scalps off to prove our allegiance and eating countless pancake breakfasts, washed down with rancid coffee. For a few seconds I thought we'd lost all that hard work at the hands of that boy, but nothing happened. We kept eating, hoping we got one free pass, or that none of the Caretakers had been watching us.

I've got high sensitivity to dream-kinesis, or what some people call 'dream-walking' abilities. I think that's the reason I was asked to participate in the ritual in the first place.

How it happened was this: one day I was sleeping, minding my own business, dream-walking without any particular purpose, when one of the Caretakers approached me in my dream-state. He told me his name was Kameel, but I don't think that's his real name. Kameel, or whoever he is, spoke to me with a clarity I'd never heard from a dream-walker before, or since.

Sometimes I wonder if I was brainwashed into joining the ritual because I was so in awe of Kameel's facility as a dream-walker or if I was easily convinced because my personal and professional life was in such a disastrous state when I met him. I'd recently lost my job at the Boar Institute, where I was an Executive Financial

Advisor. Back in those days I had no self-control. I'd dream-walk right through the middle of meetings and eventually management caught on.

After I lost my job, I was borrowing money from everyone I could, doing small but risky under-the-table finance deals, constantly afraid of getting caught. So when I met Kameel, I was ready for a change and that's exactly what he offered, plus the opportunity to use my one and only skill: dream-walking.

Kameel told me how the ritual worked. He explained the deep history of it and stressed that strict adherence to its rules would become my number one priority if I agreed to join. Then he told me the names of some of the most famous and influential people that had taken the rites before me and hinted that I could become powerful and influential, too. The ritual seemed like the answer to all of my problems, plus I crave structure, and the prospect of months of adhering to an incontrovertible set of rules finally won me over.

When I spoke to Kameel, my pledge sounded horrible, warped and extremely high-pitched. I remember waking up that morning feeling that something major had been altered and that there was no going back. From then on there was nowhere I could hide that Kameel wouldn't find me.

That was before they took my hair.

That night, after Vermont's hat fell off in the diner, I couldn't sleep. I felt worried and excited. I had to resist the urge to go into carrier pigeon mode before the chosen time. I sat on my hotel bed and flipped through a catalogue to occupy myself. I ran my hands over the glossy pages, feeling them melt through my hands, into my eye-glands. Every person that had ever touched the magazine became a portal I could see and hear through if I wanted. There was a remote quality to each of their experiences—and in my experience of their experiences—that amazed me. Every one of them had their own private obscurity that I was all of a sudden privy to, and this extra bit of dream-walking power Kameel taught me to harness in my waking state sent thrills through my feet and up into my stomach and armpits.

I could see regular curtains, regular shadows, and the unremarkable lives being lived behind them. I was totally sent, catapulted into waves of joy sensations, into fits of religious sucklage (dream-walking could be infinitely better than sex or drugs, and far more addictive). As soon as I indulged myself by entering one of those pliant, unsuspecting heads, I wanted more; at least half of my dream-walking power was occupied by this want, and that made me furious. It diminished my dream-walking powers significantly to feel so gluttonous and unfulfilled.

I did my best to brush it off, forget it, throw it all back into a body-consciousness that was constantly rippling with strange sausage-link sensations, as I slipped from one life to the next to the next to the next. The most thrilling part of dream-walking is that thin passage between lives, where all experience becomes vacant and a pure bliss vacuum carries you along. In between vessels is the purest happiness you can find, but you can't stay there. If you did, it would be worse than death, or so I've heard. All I permitted myself was one little toe tip into that nethereal bath. That would have to be enough.

That night, the state men received their packing orders from me, the carrier pigeon. The orders were simple and everyone received the same spiel: bring a clean change of clothes in a black duffel bag. But that wasn't the most important part. They went to sleep that night half-expecting to meet me there. What they didn't expect was how sharp my pigeon's beak would be when it entered their dreams. If they weren't alerted to the seriousness of the ritual via acute psychic pain, Kameel told me, then there was a chance that some of them might not take it seriously enough—a huge liability, especially the night before the most important stage.

So I made sure my entry into their dream-states hurt and left a mark they wouldn't be able to forget. Kameel had trained me well.

■

Everyone was already at the entrance to the ranch when I pulled up in my rental car. The headlights illuminated a pack of tired, disgruntled looking cowboys in identical costumes, topped with four white cowboy hats, each holding a black duffel bag.

"How'd y'all sleep?" I said, stepping out of the car,

laughing at their dejected expressions, a hollow fear creeping up inside of me.

A few of them grumbled incoherently.

"Seems like you could have picked an easier way to send a message," New Hampshire said, massaging his temples with a hand decked in cheap-looking rings.

"No," I explained, cutting him off, "packing orders have to come from the carrier pigeon, or else the ritual wouldn't work."

That was the secret phrase among us. If anyone said we had to do something or else the ritual wouldn't work, then we had to do it, no questions asked. After I said that, everyone was quiet and kept their discomfort to themselves.

Five minutes later, one of the Caretakers walked out of a field toward us. He was bald with nasty looking burn scars all over his head, and he was decked out in an impeccable black suit and tie, with shiny, wing-tipped shoes to top it all off. He didn't say anything when he approached, just unlocked the front gate and signalled for us to follow him in.

He walked in front of us into the dark field, his shiny, scarred head a beacon above his black suit. We could barely see what was under our feet: scrub brushes, some crab grass, rocks, and not much else. A few of us tripped over shadowy clumps as we walked. I was a bit disappointed. I had pictured something different for the setting of the ritual: great basalt ruins and stone archways blackened by smoke from torches passing close to the walls, as hooded people ran their calloused hands over the layers of history to steady themselves against fear of the unknown, or something. This just looked like every other empty field I'd walked or driven past in my life.

The Caretaker never looked back, never moved his gaze from the barn as we approached it, and his rigid composure amidst all of our burbling nervousness helped reinforce the gravity of what we were about to do.

No one said anything. A heavy feeling descended upon us as we walked through the field toward the barn. I recall having this extra sense that something fresh had taken over my life. That I was no longer a willing participant; my consent in being there was just an illusion, and anything that happened or was going to happen to me, was going to happen because it fit someone else's vision of the world—what was going to happen was out of my control.

We approached the barn. There was a pigpen beside it and a few pigs sleeping on their stomachs and sides. There was one pig lying on its back with its feet in the air. Vermont laughed and pointed it out. The Caretaker looked at him so sternly, it immediately shut him up, then the Caretaker gestured with his bald, fucked-up head for us to get inside the barn.

It was a big barn and there was only one light bulb on in the whole place. The rest of the interior was buried in deep blackness. I couldn't see through it to the other side. A few wooden poles supported what I guessed was a second level and there was hay covering the ground except in one spot, directly under the light bulb, where it had been cleared away to form a circle of bare cement.

The Caretaker told us to drop our duffel bags and stand inside the circle. Nobody spoke. We all got in underneath the single light bulb. The circle was tight, there was enough room for us all, but it was impossible for our arms not to touch once we were inside. The single light bulb cast shadows under our hats so that our faces were obscured from each other. Silence and darkness permeated all around.

The Caretaker ordered us to undress, just like that: "Undress," he said and so we did.

For some privacy, or so he didn't have to see us in the flesh, or because if he didn't turn around while we undressed and turn off the light, then the ritual wouldn't work, the Caretaker turned around and turned off the only light in the barn.

We shuffled out of our cowboy costumes and stood naked in the circle. Then the Caretaker turned the light back on. I was mortified. Under the single light bulb stood six naked men including myself, without our hats on, each of our burned scalps out in the open for the first time, marking us as initiates of the sacred ritual.

The Caretaker walked around and inspected our heads to make sure that we were true initiates of the ritual. If we hadn't already felt exposed and vulnerable before that, we realized that while we were undressing, a half-dozen pigs had gathered noiselessly and formed a circle around us in the dark. When the light came on, their snouts and eyes flared as though they were judging us or sizing us up. I remember they were hairier than I realized pigs could be. The way they snorted and bared their teeth at us made me feel deeply uncomfortable in my vulnerable state, and I believe I caught one of them winking at me.

"Now we can start," the Caretaker said, just like that, receding into the darkness once again. "The pigs will root out any unworthy candidates amongst you. You should only be afraid if your purposes here are impure. If they aren't, relax and enjoy the ride. If they are, prepare for a reckoning."

With that, the Caretaker switched off the only source of light in the barn. From the darkness he ordered us to hold each other's hands and under no circumstances were we to let them go. I fumbled for the hands of Tex and New Hampshire on either side of me. The pigs were beginning to run in circles behind us. Convulsions ripped through our circle as their speed increased.

"Don't look behind you," the Caretaker commanded to us from out of the shadows.

It became harder to keep my hands around Tex's and New Hampshire's. We were being pulled apart by the whirlwind of stampeding pigs behind us and the seizures going through the circle became a test of strength. I thought we were going to lift off the ground and for a second, I think we may have.

Someone started yammering. It sounded like they were standing at the far end, running up close to my face, and then quickly receding to the back of the barn again. I wondered if it was my own voice become detached from my body that I was hearing. The voice yammered and zoomed. The sounds it made were nonsense. I could feel someone's breath on my face, but I couldn't tell whose.

The circle was wrenched from side to side and the hands holding mine became slick with sweat. A strong wind rushed up my back from the whirlwind of pigs behind us, then the yammering voice reached an insane pitch and, for a moment, I could kind of understand what it was saying:

> One of you has been a pig impostor all your life. One of you is returning to your rightful pig flock with every gust of this pig wind. You feel it touch you and kiss you in your true pigness. You want to nose around with us. You want to run around and bound on all fours with us. Come nudge rocks out of the ground and reel around in mud and bugs with us. Whoever it is must break the circle now. Whoever it is must break the circle now. Whoever it is must come with us. Your little pig clothes are all in order. You're going to be wearing a beautiful pig dress in this new pig world. You'll be leading a pig's life and you'll have pig's eyes to see it through. Whoever it is, you are of the pig and from the depths of your true pigness, you will become aware of your false costume. With every breath of pig wind, you will shuffle off your false costume and come with us.

RATS NEST

The pig wind became a pig gale. I didn't think I'd be able to hold on much longer. I started doubting my reasons for pledging myself to the ritual. I wanted to go home and dream-walk through the rest of my miserable life, get by on shady under-the-table finance deals, and never pay anyone back what I owed.

Then the voice stopped bombarding us; the pig wind ceased blowing and the circle became more relaxed. I could hear the pigs shuffle out of the barn and there was a stretch of time in which everything was quiet and our sweaty palms remained locked.

The Caretaker announced that he was going to turn the light back on and we were allowed to let go of each other's hands.

We stood in front of each other under the painful light of the single bulb, naked, panting, looking at each other but trying not to at the same time. I remember Tex's sweaty pot-belly heaving from the strain and Colorado looking at the ground, cupping his balls. New Hampshire was shaking his head. Vermont was gone.

I looked around, thinking that he might've been hiding, or thrown behind us by the gale. Then I realized, as the others must have already, that Vermont had left with the pigs. Our circle had been broken after all.

The Caretaker asked us to stay quiet and get into our changes of clothes. We could leave the way we came, he said. That was it for the night.

We met at the pancake house the next morning. I'd barely slept and I was the last to arrive. From the parking lot I could see that Vermont was there with them; his white rental car was in the parking lot and he was sitting in the booth with the others like he had many times before.

I sat in my rental car in the parking lot of the pancake house with the engine turned off, and thought about how I felt about everything that had happened up until that point. I didn't feel in control of the situation and I wasn't sure what my role was now that we'd been initiated into the circle of pigs. I didn't reach any satisfying conclusions, but I became worried that the state men would see me sitting there. So, I waved my hand over the door handle and permitted myself to leave the car.

Over breakfast, all the state men, including Vermont, acted like nothing out of the ordinary had occurred. Tex was ornery as usual. New Hampshire was paranoid. He scanned the room to see if we were being surveilled. I didn't understand what was going on. I kept looking at Vermont for some clue about what had happened to him. Something about the five of us sitting there, waiting to be served, just like we had in the past, made me feel nervous. Was this still part of the ritual, I wondered?

Our pancakes were served and Tex passed his hand over the table. I looked around to see if any of them noticed how strange this all was, but everyone was avoiding making eye contact with me and pretending to be interested in their pancake breakfasts instead.

RATS NEST

The same little boy from the day before popped up in the booth behind us. I recognized his mom as well. The little boy smiled at me. I tipped my cowboy hat at him and he bashed with excitement at the cushion next to Vermont's cowboy hat. His mom swatted at him gently and missed and the boy disappeared behind the cushion, while New Hampshire cracked some awkward jokes.

"I bet you can't wait to get back home where everyone wears hats like this?" he nodded at Tex. "I'm going to give mine to a charity for short people," New Hampshire said, patting the top of his hat. "Wearing one of these makes a person feel tall."

There was a crash of utensils on ceramic as something hit the table; it was Vermont's hat falling off his head and landing on his plate again. This time the little boy hid behind the booth, but not very well. I could see a wisp of his light brown hair sticking up over the edge of the cushion and a balled-up, pudgy little hand; it wasn't the little boy we were looking at though, it was Vermont.

With his hat knocked off, we could see his scalp; it was no longer a mess of scars and burns like the rest of ours. The top of his head was still bald, but it was pristine. It was so smooth and perfect-looking, I thought it might be a bald cap but, from where I sat, I could also see some brown stubble emerging and even a vein or two, so it was his real head after all. No burns. No scars.

"I'm really sorry. That's the second time he's done that isn't it?" the boy's mom said to Vermont over the seat cushion.

"No ma'am. That was the first," Vermont said, not looking at her. Oblivious.

"Can I give you some money to get it cleaned?" she asked.

"That won't be necessary," Vermont said, looking over his shoulder at the boy's mom and turning back around to take a sip of his coffee, as if nothing significant had transpired.

"Eric, I want you to apologize—" the boy's mother said.

There was a pause and then the boy's disembodied voice squeaked from the other side of the booth: "Saww-rree."

"That all right," Vermont said. Then he saw all of us staring at him. "What?" he asked, sensing that something was wrong. "I won't need it much longer, anyway."

New Hampshire snapped his head to the side to look at me and then at Tex and Colorado. I nodded my assent, as did Colorado, then Tex passed his hand over the table, releasing us from breakfast. New Hampshire jumped up from his seat, crawled across Colorado while taking a knife out his belt, and stabbed Vermont in the neck. He sawed it out backwards, then rammed it back in. New Hampshire repeated this action five more times until Vermont's neck was thoroughly bloody and slashed. Vermont squealed, pig-like. His blood sprayed on the table and on the booth in front of us. His legs kicked out from under him, he gurgled some more, and fought to get free, but New Hampshire just kept pulling the knife out and ramming it back in. It was a dirty technique and a bloody mess, but it did the trick.

Everyone in the restaurant ran out except us, the state men: Texas, Colorado, New Hampshire, the recently deceased body of Vermont, and myself.

The sky was almost completely black when I pulled up to the ranch. As I got out of my air-conditioned rental car, the humidity was unbearable. I lit a cigarette and waited for the Caretaker to appear.

When he finally did, the sky was rumbling with the first phases of what promised to be a damaging storm.

"I have the body," I said to the Caretaker, not knowing how else to put it.

The Caretaker just nodded and let me in. I drove slowly past the empty pigpen and waited for the others to arrive. By the time they parked in front of the barn, fat drops of rain were splattering my windshield.

Colorado and Texas helped me get Vermont's body out of the trunk and into the barn. We'd wrapped it in a hotel bed sheet now dripping with blood. The Caretaker told us to lay it in the cement circle surrounded by a donut of hay under the solitary light bulb under which we had stood the night before. Once we'd laid the shrouded body in the circle, the Caretaker told us to get out. All of his attention was now focused on the body of Vermont and the circle of pigs that had just assembled around him. We backed out of the barn into the rain and into our respective cars.

By this time it sounded like rocks were falling out of the sky onto my roof and windshield. As I sat listening to it, I wondered if it would put me to sleep. Then I felt something in the backseat with me and heard Kameel's clear, subliminal voice in my head. He ordered me to get each of the state men out of their cars and into the barn. I wasn't allowed to use physical force and I wasn't to say a word to any of them out loud.

He told me he was testing my dream-walking

abilities and my loyalty to the ritual at the same time. He informed me that, if I didn't obey his orders, then the ritual wouldn't work. He didn't need to threaten me, though. I was completely under his spell, just like the first time we met.

I looked out my passenger-side window at the other three cars. I was parked next to Tex. He was looking out his windshield at the barn. As I closed my eyes and concentrated all my energy on him, his head slumped to the side, his hat hit the door frame and fell off, he moved back to the centre of the windshield again and then winged his bald head hard off the passenger-side window, crumpled onto the steering wheel, twitched, opened his door and fell out, face first in the mud, his legs still inside the car.

He struggled with me some more. Tex was a strong motherfucker and harder to control than I had anticipated, so I moved to the passenger seat to get a better hold on him. I could feel Kameel in the backseat, just behind my lowered eyelids, judging my dream-walking abilities. I eventually positioned myself inside of Tex and got an unbreakable hold on his involuntary responses. He began crawling on all fours through the mud and rain toward the barn.

Kameel told me to focus my energies on Colorado and New Hampshire next. I got out of my car, slogged through the rain and jumped into Tex's rental to get a closer read on the other two state men.

Colorado was wiping the inside of his windshield with the sleeve of his shirt. He craned his neck to see who or what the mound of clothes crawling toward the barn was. Then he turned in his seat to look at me, narrowed his eyes and wrinkled his forehead, already bracing for a fight. I eventually got inside him by setting up a decoy: I triggered his sleep reflex and, while he was fighting that off, I took control of his motor functions. He started jumping up and down in his seat like a frog and flailing his arms. After an agonizing but brief struggle, I was able to get him out of the car, too, his head cocked at an angle, eyes staring straight at me, enraged.

Outside in the rain, he started yelling at me. I couldn't hear what he was saying. I could just see his mouth open wide as the torrents of rain swallowed up the sound, his body tense and shaking as he waddled against his will in the direction of the barn.

New Hampshire was easier to control than the others, maybe because he was more willing to go. As soon as I got into Colorado's car and hijacked New Hampshire's nervous system, he opened his door and walked with purpose towards the barn, as the other two crawled and shuffled behind him. When they were all inside, the doors of the barn were closed and I was alone in Colorado's car with the rain coming down hard.

I waited for a long time, not knowing what was going on. I could see that the light was off, but I couldn't see or hear anything else. Kameel was silent, but I knew he was still inside, keeping an eye on me. I started wondering what I was doing there. What part was I playing? Why had I joined the ritual, I asked myself, and what did I want to get from it now? Then Kameel moved and spoke inside of me. He told me that I didn't need to know what was happening inside the barn, or anywhere else, for that matter. He said that I should be proud to serve the Caretakers of the ritual and to help maintain the order. To wish for anything else, Kameel said, was treacherous, and could warrant a severe punishment if I wasn't careful.

I remained quiet and tried not to let him know how much I resented his patronizing tone. I believed even less in the ritual after that. Were the others being inducted into some secret rite, while I was parked outside like a chauffeur? Kameel didn't say anything further.

We sat together in silence while the rain continued to fall.

Eventually the barn doors opened and the Caretaker walked towards me through the rain. I rolled my window down and he asked me to move the other vehicles. From where I was parked, I tried to see inside the barn, but it was too dark. So I am the chauffeur after all, I thought.

After I moved the cars, the Caretaker said I wasn't needed anymore and I drove to the hotel, feeling deeply despondent.

That night Kameel visited me again. He told me to show up at the pancake house, at the same time as usual, the next morning. He said the others would be there as well. He told me that this would be our last breakfast together, and following the completion of our meal, the ritual would be complete.

I wanted to ask him what was going to happen and

what it was all about, but when I spoke those words in my warped high-pitched dream-walker's voice, there was no one around to hear them.

■

The next morning I drove from my hotel to the pancake house with the sole purpose of finding out what had happened the day before. They were all there when I arrived, except Vermont, and they were all wearing the same old cowboy outfit, including the white cowboy hats we had always worn.

That's when I realized I'd left my hat in the hotel room. I raised my hands to touch the still-fresh burns on the top of my bald head. I must've been really out of it to forget something that important. I considered sneaking away and going back to the hotel to get it, but it was too late, the remaining state men were looking at me from the booth with horrified expressions.

"I know," I said, squeezing into the booth beside Colorado.

"How could you forget it?" New Hampshire hissed.

Tex put his face in his hands and Colorado scanned the room to see if any of the Caretakers or their spies were there, observing us. Sure enough, the same little boy and his mom were in the booth in front of ours. The state men must've ordered before I arrived because the waitress appeared, balancing a brown plastic tray with all of our plates on top of it, not long after I sat down.

As she put the plates in front of us, the three

remaining state men stared at me and my disgusting, bald head, with charred skin and sparse clumps of hair for everyone in the restaurant to see. I looked back at them, and realized that I no longer cared what happened to them or the ritual. As soon as they were in front of me, I dove into my plate of pancakes without letting Tex do his hand waving thing. I believe I even mouthed the words, 'fuck you,' at him as I did, and he stared back at me with a look of disgust.

The pancakes tasted fine and nothing fell from the sky. The state men were all too intent on my transgressions to notice the little boy behind them making a grab for Tex's hat. He knocked it off Tex's head and it landed on a plate of recently syrupped pancakes.

Everyone looked at Tex. Without his hat on, we could see that he was sporting a bountiful new head of hair—a brunette pompadour with the lustre and coif of a man twenty years' younger—growing naturally on top of his head. Tex looked at New Hampshire, as though he was waiting for a signal or a word about what to do next. Then he lifted his hat off the plate and turned, with his exquisite new head of hair, to look at the boy.

The boy was frozen, staring at our terrifying table: two men in white hats, one with a ridiculous new pompadour that didn't suit him, and me with my badly burnt scalp, covered in shiny black scabs.

Tex stared hard at the boy until there was a loud shucking sound and the boy's head popped off his body; it launched off his neck in a short, smooth arc. The boy's headless body fell backwards and his free-floating head hit the wall at the back of the restaurant, ricocheted off of it, and landed on another customer's table, where it knocked a glass of orange juice over and came to rest on a plate of waffles.

Outside the sky became very dark and the ground began to rumble. That's when I knew that the ritual was definitely real and that I had ruined it because I was the impure one, not Vermont.

I started to laugh at the exact same moment something started to scream very loudly in my ear.

ALWAYS DARK

In a one-room cabin, in the middle of an always dark forest, under a perpetually full moon that spins in circles above the roof, a mother brushes something that looks like paste through her youngest daughter's hair. Her older sister sits at a dining room table and pours milk into a bowl. She pushes the bowl in front of a cat, roughly six feet long, with gossamer white fur, sitting at the table, looking sullen and bored.

Martens play in the moonlight outside the cabin. They nose big black bugs out of the ground and take them into their mouths.

A woman on a motorcycle drives up a long, dark stretch of road that cuts through the always dark forest toward the cabin, the beam of light on the front of her bike a V-shaped mouth that envelops everything in its path.

The mother and her daughters hear the motorcycle approach and start to scramble around inside the cabin. They open cupboards and doors and search frantically under the table and chairs. The cat looks at them blankly, as it laps the bowl of milk.

The three women continue to clamber through the cabin as the motorcycle woman gets close, the bright front lamp of the bike visible to them now through the thick growth of the always dark forest. They find what they were looking for in the kitchen cupboard: three wide ceramic masks, which they attach to their faces with the aid of a rough piece of twine, pulled tight around the head, and tied at the back in a bow.

Each mask is identical: flat, white and hard like a dinner plate, with two eyeholes and a mouth hole drilled into it. The mother attaches her own mask and then helps her youngest daughter attach hers, gripping the twine behind her brown locks and tightening it with a couple strong pulls.

The grand cat finishes its bowl of milk and blinks twice, as it enjoys doing. The three women stand in a row, as though awaiting orders, each with a white dinner plate with eyeholes and a mouth hole drilled into it attached to their faces. The cat gets down from its seat at the kitchen table, stretches its back, curls up in front of a black pot-belly stove with a fire burning inside of it, and closes its eyes for a snooze.

The three women have to manoeuvre past its broad shaggy frame to draw three metal pokers from the stove. The pokers have been resting in hot coals for hours and as the mother and the oldest daughter take them out, each one pops and glows. The mother hands her youngest daughter a poker of her own. The little girl grips it proudly with both hands and smiles, as the glowing orange point warms her face through the hard porcelain of her mask.

The motorcycle woman comes to a stop, the engine of the bike still running, the V of the front lamp swallowing the front of the cabin, bathing it in chimeric yellow light. The motorcycle woman removes her helmet and turns off the engine, but not the front lamp; it stays on as she steps off the bike. Her heavy boots crunch gravel, dried ferns, and beetles, and a pack of martens scurry into the safety of the always dark forest with live black bugs squirming around inside each of their mouths.

The driver of the motorcycle has a ruddy sack slung over her shoulders, which she removes as she advances toward the cabin. She stands in front of the door now, her stance wide, and yells to the three women on the other side.

The front door of the cabin hurls open, the lamp on the front of the motorcycle shatters, and the always dark forest returns to utter blackness, as three hot pokers emerge from the doorway, like the three glowing eyes of some mythical beast. The motorcycle woman doesn't break her stride. She opens the sack, lifts a slab of purple, quivering meat from out of it, and holds it up for the women inside the cabin to see by the light of their simultaneously gleaming pokers.

The women raise their pokers and cheer at the sight of the elusive, purple meat. They had been waiting for this moment, growing hungry, worried that the motorcycle woman might never arrive, or if she did, that she might arrive empty-handed. The motorcycle woman tosses the rare hunk of game into the cabin. It lands on the dirty, wooden floorboards and begins quivering and jerking spasmodically, as though it's making a desperate attempt to escape.

RATS NEST

The three women pounce on the meat slab and keep it pinned to the dirty floorboards with the tips of their ever-hot pokers, pressing down, puncturing the flesh; sparks spurt up and collide with the solid ware of their masks. The motorcycle woman walks past the preoccupied women—she enters the cabin tentatively and surveys the impoverished interior: a warped and weathered dining room table; a bench and two chairs; the black, pot-belly stove, chipped and old, in front of which the big, fluffy cat lays wrapped in heat; a rocking chair; and two threadbare cushions nearby.

Outside, the trees of the always dark forest continue to sway and the perpetually full moon continues to spin and revolve above the roof, and the martens—now safely ensconced in the security of the forest—enjoy their dinner of black bugs, which they crunch happily in their mouths.

The motorcycle woman looks over at the three hungry women, who laugh and cry loudly as they cook their beautiful bounty. Steam and smoke rise from the once purple and quaking husk, now baked and pinned to the floor. The oldest daughter giggles as it turns a shade of light brown in front of her. Her giggles echo inside her mask. They wake the slumbering cat giant who looks up at the motorcycle woman, sniffs at the air now thick with a heady stench of broiled meat, and licks its chops in expectation of the immanent feast.

The oldest daughter retrieves a serving plate from the kitchen cupboard and brings it over to the doorway. Her mother spears the meat with her poker, hoists it onto the plate, then she and her oldest daughter carry it over to the dining room table. The steamy meat is no longer purple but a delicious brown with black, burnt ends.

The youngest daughter stands at the motorcycle woman's feet. She stares up at her inquisitively through the eyeholes in her face protector. The motorcycle woman smiles, kneels down and unties the rough twine holding the dinner plate to the littlest one's head. The mother, as she carves the meat with a sharp, serrated knife, watches the motorcycle woman lift her youngest daughter off the ground, and seat her on the bench alongside the dining room table.

The cat rises up from the floor and arches its back. As it does, the mother places the carved meat in front of the cat's favorite chair and the remaining three women sit down on the bench . The cat curls its voluminous body into its chair across the table from the women and directly in front of the ample serving of steak. The entire portion is roughly the size of an adult human's back, carved expertly by the mother into serviceable chunks, which the cat sniffs, and then carefully, and thoughtfully licks.

The cat takes its time before delivering its appraisal of the feast. It licks one of its large paws and lays it on the table. Its giant claws emerge; the tips lodge themselves in the well-worn tabletop and then retract back into its foot pads. The claws emerge, retract, and emerge again, twice more.

The youngest daughter giggles and covers her eyes at the sight of the cat's performance.

RATS NEST

Then the cat begins to purr, a heavy rumble that causes the table and the bench that the four women are seated upon, to vibrate. The purr contains within it a message and each of the women, in turn, understands what it means: that 'the meat is good,' the big cat approves, and that now they may eat.

All four women lunge madly at the chubby victuals arranged by the mother so appealingly across the length of the serving plate. They eat with their hands; mumbles of enjoyment fill the one room cabin in the middle of the always dark forest, under the perpetually spinning moon, as the cat continues to purr harmoniously and lap up the meat juice from in between its two enormous paws.

CONTENT WORMS

'Outbreak of content worms in Unit 9,' the mechanical voice said from the one-way speaker, then a red light flashed, signalling that the message had ended. Providence pushed a button to indicate he had received it, fumbled the receiver back into its cradle, and schlepped open the folding doors of the com-booth. He'd been working the same beat for 33 years. The alarms were all rote. He no longer cared. He used to think that, by doing his job as a peace officer, and later on as a math detective, he helped make the world a bit better, or at least kept it from sliding further into chaos, but those feelings changed, ten years ago, when his wife and daughter were sucked into an ether well; basically a wormhole into the ether realm.

They were rescued, but they were rescued too late. When someone falls into a well or they are exposed to pure ether for too long, they come back a vape— just the physical husk of a person—the rest of them remains in the ether realm where, some people believe, their physical form is manipulated by invisible and malevolent creatures.

Providence didn't buy it though. He thought that he could go into the ether realm and get back what it had taken from him. So, one day, while out on a routine call, he stumbled upon a fresh, burgeoning ether well that had yet to be reported. He sized up his odds, said his prayers, so to speak, plugged his nose, and jumped inside. Three weeks later, they found him, raving mad but, by some miracle, he hadn't turned vape.

Providence became known as the first person to return from the ether relatively unscathed. He even brought back something with him—an unbreakable conviction that the physical world was being controlled and predetermined by creatures inside the ether—and the real kicker, he told people, what he'd learned from his experiences there, including his inability to rescue his wife and daughter's remains—was that he alone had been chosen to lead a singularly futile and irredeemable life. Ever since his rescue, he knew that, wherever he went, and whatever he did there, whatever the days laid out in front of him, and whatever illusions of good, or merely satisfactory fortune he seemed to be enjoying in his paltry excuse for a life, he'd been allowed to return from the ether realm intact for one reason: to be the recipient of some extended and strenuous torture. He wanted to stick around just long enough to find out why.

The part of the city where Providence worked had no street lights and the houses and offices kept their power turned off at night to conserve electricity. Providence stumbled through the darkness by memory, putting one soiled white sneaker in front of the other. A vape creature shuffled along the sidewalk behind him, breathing a tethered green cloud from its mouth. Providence registered its presence, but didn't pay close attention. He hated wasting time on those wretched things and there were more of them in the city every day as more people fell victim to the ether wells.

But this particular vape creature had an ulterior motive. It excreted a green jelly from its shrivelled lips, which, as it got closer, it gobbed it onto the back of Providence's cheap windbreaker. This stinking splat landed on Providence's collar, slathered his neck and stuck to his cheek. He turned to face the vape; its green cloud of breath, and the jelly it excreted were harmless, but approaching a non-vape, touching them, breathing on them, or excreting jelly on them, were strictly prohibited according to the law that Providence was paid a meager wage to uphold.

Providence took a gun from his windbreaker pocket and pointed it at the creature. He hoped it would just go away. But the vape just stood there, shaking and salivating, as though coming to terms with the misery of its own existence in the midst of their exchange.

Another green breath emerged from its mouth, a milky puff that floated up into the sky—a sign that it was heavily etherized, mostly out of the physical world and not an immediate threat. Providence laughed at the gross futility of the vape creature and wiped the slime from the back of his neck. The green stuff smelled like rotting fish but Providence's mind was too dulled by pills, booze, and a lifetime of vile experiences to mind.

The vape creature took a few more steps toward him, a clear provocation according to the law, so Providence shot it twice. It staggered as both green slime and ether escaped from a new hole in its stomach. Then it fell, as more green gas escaped from its face.

Another day, another dead vape, Providence thought. He returned the pistol to his windbreaker pocket and continued walking toward his car. A small crowd of civilians gathered to watch the vape creature's last gasps. Soon, Providence wouldn't be able to remember what had happened, only that his standard issue revolver was two bullets lighter.

His real concern lay on the other side of the block in Unit 9, a public hotel where an infestation of content worms had just been reported. This meant that real people were at risk. If content worms were allowed to infest a building for too long, they would eventually open an ether well that could start sucking people in. Providence couldn't let what happened to his wife and daughter happen to others. He never talked about what he'd seen in the ether, what had wrecked him and changed him so irrevocably in there. Everyone assumed it was too painful to talk about and they were right.

Providence drove the short distance to Unit 9. A bunch of firefighters, paramedics, cops and civilians stood around the parking lot, looking agitated, their bodies coloured red, yellow and blue by the flashing lights of the emergency vehicles.

Providence approached the two nearest math detectives and lit a cigarette as sparks ignited inside Unit 9 like flashes of frenetic brain activity.

"Bernays, Dayroulx…" Providence said, chewing the end of his cigarette.

Bernays and Dayroulx looked at him like he was a dog in a tuxedo or someone who had pulled a large working light bulb from out of his ear.

"I don't believe it," Dayroulx said, squinting at Providence.

"No way!" said Bernays, a bit more animated, causing Providence to look away in disgust. He wasn't accustomed to, nor was he in the mood for being scrutinized or talked to in loud cheerful tones, especially Bernays' slimy impersonation of cheer.

"No way!" Bernays repeated and put a greasy hand on Providence's plastic windbreaker. "But he feels real!"

Providence moved away from Bernays' pawing. He mouthed the last of his sodden filter and let it topple out of his mouth onto the ground, where it smoked some more before fizzling out.

"I've been fooled by ether fakes before," said Dayroulx and blew a puff of cigarette smoke in Providence's face, then looked around the other side to make sure it didn't pass straight through him, which it didn't.

"The man. The myth. The mostly real skin," Bernays said with more annoying gusto and reached out to pat Providence down again.

Providence pulled away and otherwise ignored them both. He studied the upper levels of the Unit 9 hotel where the lights continued to flash on and off in rapid succession. He felt the familiar pull: That way leads to suffering and tragedy, the kind of understanding that can only be got by agony, Providence thought.

"I'm going in," he said, devoid of enthusiasm.

RATS NEST

Bernays and Dayroulx looked at each other. They weren't sure who or what Providence had become since he jumped into that ether well, but he didn't seem to care what happened to himself anymore.

"You sure?" Dayroulx said but he was already walking away.

They both stifled a laugh as they watched Providence's bowling-pin-shaped body stumble toward the entrance of Unit 9, the flag of his comb-over coming undone, flapping in the wind as though waving goodbye, his soiled sneakers and windbreaker a fitting uniform for his increasingly infectious lack of hope.

When Providence opened the ground floor doors and stepped inside Unit 9, he felt the atmosphere change. The lobby was dark except for a lamp on the concierge's desk that seemed to be fighting to stay alive. Providence stuck his right index finger in his mouth, then took it back out. Before he could perform that rudimentary test, he noticed his movements were more sluggish than usual, and with his wet index finger, he guesstimated that the atmosphere was at least two degrees denser inside than out.

This new level of sluggishness he was feeling would have been comedic to him had time not been such an issue. It was getting harder to breathe and if he was going to find whatever it was he felt fated to find inside Unit 9, he needed to find it fast. Eventually the whole place would become an ether well, yet another portal to that horrible realm, in a city already riddled with them.

Providence licked his lips in slow motion. The air tasted like burnt marshmallows. He could literally follow his nose to the place where he suspected the infestation of content worms originated from. With great effort he crossed the lumpy linoleum of the hotel lobby. His middle-aged smoker's body heaved slowly up the stairs to the second floor. Within seconds he was soaked with sweat, his red pulpy face glistening, his comb-over reduced to a few spindly threads tracing weak lines across his forehead.

When he reached the second floor he knew that he would not have the energy to descend those stairs and exit Unit 9 to safety ever again. This is where I'm going to die, he thought and looked around at the peeling yellow wallpaper, the mostly broken lights and the blood red carpet littered with plaster, stuffing, and hair, and then he thought again, I guess that makes sense.

He made a shape with his mouth like he was saying the word 'bake' or had a hair stuck in his throat. The air was so thick with content worms that breathing it in was like trying to swallow a piece of dry toast whole. This was the expression he was wearing when Mantra first caught sight of him in the hallway, on the second floor of the Unit 9 hotel, and she would never forget it.

"I've been waiting for this," she said out loud, getting up out of the once comfortable, now gutted wing-backed lobby chair and floated across the five feet of red carpet to situate herself in front of Providence. She was wearing a black cloak up to her chin and only her face was visible; though round and bright, it wasn't made of skin at all. Her eyes stood out from her unmoving visage, hard and uniformly black; her cloak shimmered and reflected in the warm glow of the hallway like velvet with a delicate finish.

Providence fingered his fat throat as she approached, trying to undo a button, anything that might help him take one last breath.

"Poor Providence," she said, "you need to stay alive a while longer so you can hear what I have to tell you." She took his hand in hers and led him into the nearest room. Her cloak flickered in and out of the perceptible world, an indication of an otherwise invisible tether—her connection back to the ether realm where she was from.

Providence rolled his eyes and fell onto the hotel bed. He gasped and writhed on the blue duvet, his face purple. From his oxygen-starved perspective, it looked as though black discs were falling from the ceiling and landing directly onto his eyeballs. He tried to brush them off. ⟩

Mantra disappeared for a second and came back with a vape creature in tow. It looked complacent, a bubble of green ether tethered to its mouth like a green buoy alerting no one of its whereabouts.

Mantra said a few words Providence couldn't make out and then the vape creature bent over and exhaled a sticky green cloud into his ear. He recoiled but wasn't strong enough to fight the vape creature off. He rolled over on his side as his mouth filled with the taste of blood and mould. Providence felt his airways open almost immediately and then the pressure in his chest and brain began to dissolve. A trail of green vapour drifted out of his mouth and hung in a little damp sack above his head. He rolled back over and watched as the vape creature waddled back into the shadows of the room and was replaced by Mantra's solid black eyes staring down at him.

She began telling him the story she had travelled from the ether realm to tell him. But his brain couldn't process that complexity of information anymore. He'd gone too long without oxygen, and with the limited cognition the vapour flowing through his system afforded him, he could only make out simple words:

> ...stone-ud, ice fur, lantern, grave-ud, made, full-height, ud-solid door, warm die, rose, glass shade nod, winter, torture, great fur-ud, at any rate, sacred old demands, finger blows, nod, agree, valley of complex equipment, whistle crawl, die, oil, machine, knowledge, tongue bed, set in motion, nod nod, vibration-ud, ud-chain of, unstable, higher veils, spike sheep, machine-ud, drawback, effort, nod, the slowly-ud, blood , walking, legible, actual officer-ud, interval deciphered, wheel, surprise, face-parts-ud, help, wound, shoulder dip, edge, blindness, strap, alarm, turning-point, in chains, bottomless stairs, boat, grave, house, keel, foreign, dig, old night basement-ud, beard, shiny solvent, wax, deep low room, sign of feet, water, water needles, waters, back gear, nod, ud, ud-solid...

RATS NEST

Eventually Providence lost the ability to recognize words completely. They became isolated sounds, devoid of semantic content, and a giant smile appeared on his face as most of him migrated to the ether. He found what he'd been looking for, but it had nothing to do with Mantra's story.

"Nod if you agree," Mantra kept saying, "nod if you agree."

Her story concerned the intricate workings of fate in the physical world—the predetermined design that had guided Providence for most of his life—and the plans that she and her people had to take control of both realms by way of the ether wells.

Providence lay on his back, a cloud of milky green vapour tethered to his mouth, his eyes staring into oblivion. Mantra stood above him, a round, skinless face with black, opaque eyes, as more vape creatures filed into the room. The air in Unit 9 had reached maximum density. No human being could survive there; only ether-based creatures like Mantra, the vape creatures, and now Providence, could survive in an atmosphere like that.

Providence got up from the bed. He drooled and shuffled and found a place to stand in the shadows of the Unit 9 hotel room with the other vape creatures (each of them with a milky green cloud hovering above them like an extra, half-formed head) and awaited Mantra's orders.

HORST

Horst saved stacks of his old notebooks and found himself looking through them when he couldn't sleep. On one particular night, restless, grappling with a problem he couldn't articulate, Horst found himself in his office, once again, sliding his hand under a pile of old notebooks and pulling out the one closest to the bottom. The cover was marbled, black and white, with a space blanked out to write a name and subject. Wedged between the cardboard covers and in between some of the ruled pages were some cat hairs and dust balls. He plucked these out and started turning through the pages.

The handwriting inside was familiar but noticeably different from his handwriting in the present. There was something looser, fatter and, he hated to admit it, duller about the handwriting he saw on the cheap notebook paper in front of him. This was probably his handwriting from five or six years ago, he guessed. Looking at those particular notes, he realized that he had become less forgiving of himself since writing them.

He flipped through a few more pages without focusing on what was there. He turned a few more pages absentmindedly and then stopped. This was usually the point in his insomniac's routine when he'd turn on the TV, or eat something, but this time he remained seated, holding the notebook open in front of him. Something he had observed on the periphery of one of the pages had alerted his subconscious. He wasn't sure what it could be, considering he hadn't been paying any attention, but the feeling was that something had arrived, asking to be attended to—scrutinizing him at the same time—and it wouldn't go away.

Horst studied the open page in front of him. There were some lazy sentence fragments, a few failed attempt at a paragraph, and somewhere toward the margin on the left hand page, a clump of hastily written words that read, 'the column of air,' underlined. Even though those words were written in handwriting that was consistent, even identical, to the handwriting throughout the rest of the notebook, Horst knew, without a doubt, that those words had been written by someone else.

And the longer he stared at them, the longer he let them permeate his brain meat through his eyeballs, the more he became convinced that those words exerted a power over him that he could not escape. Horst knew that by discovering those words—and in the slow recognition that had begun to writhe around inside him about what they meant—he had just initiated the annihilation sequence that would come to abolish his sweet miserable life.

Horst had some idea about who might've written those alien words. He suddenly remembered another time when he'd felt similarly invaded and demolished, but the time had passed and he'd either repressed it or rationalized it away. Either way, those words from his old notebook stimulated a once forgotten memory of a party he had thrown back in his college days. Horst was drunk, lying on the floor of his bedroom, while his roommates and their friends yelled over dance music playing loudly on the stereo. He writhed on the floor, trying to find a position that would stop the room from spinning around him. He eventually manoeuvred himself to a sitting position, his back against the frame and mattress of his bed. From there he could see his reflection in a floor-length mirror nailed to the back of the bedroom door. But the person reflected in the mirror was someone Horst had never seen before. He felt his body seize up in alarm. The intruder he saw before him was covered in chunks of lumpy, coagulated blood, unrecognizable goo that could have been intestines, and stray bits of gory viscera. Worst of all, Horst knew in his petrified state, that these were his own raw innards displayed on the outer form of the invader that he was seeing, and in the whiplash of this recognition, Horst threw up and lost consciousness. The invader in the mirror remained seated and calmly tasted what they found there.

Horst woke on the floor of his kitchen. Notebooks were spread all over it. He could see the ruled pages of one lying next to him and it was filled with what looked like new handwriting. The handwriting was familiar, and yet Horst knew, once again, that it was not his own handwriting that he was reading. Those notes expressed thoughts he'd never had and the emotional register they were written in was wrong. Whoever had written them must have been in a maniacal state, not a mental condition Horst was familiar with before reading them. The person who wrote those notes had been so full of confidence, so self-assured and self-possessed, that they read as though they could go on in their exegesis forever; and from the litter of open notebooks covered in ink surrounding Horst on the linoleum floor of his kitchen; and the eight or so hours of his unaccounted for activity that had just passed, it looked as though they had.

The notebooks made numerous references to 'the column of air,' underlined, and 'the vessel,' not underlined. In fact, that word 'vessel' was repeated so many times, it started to look unreal to him. Horst's body and head throbbed in multiple places as he read. Then he started to feel porous. Nothing around him felt solid and he realized that either he was melting into the linoleum, or it was melting into him. He pushed down on the floor, in an effort to get up and leave, to go someplace where he felt more like himself, and less like a sieve with a person falling through it. One of his hands slid off the pages of a notebook, as he tried and failed to lift himself up off the tiles.

"All these fucking words," Horst babbled out loud. But what he heard when he spoke didn't make any sense.

The words that came out of his mouth, that reverberated in the middle of the kitchen, in the empty apartment, didn't sound like a human voice at all.

They sounded like a mix of animal cries fed through a distortion pedal and a wah-wah pedal, excruciatingly loud. He was unable to stand. Whatever was responsible for writing those notes had also hi-jacked his nervous system. All he could do was flip over onto his back, flail around, and spit. And as he spat, some globs of it landed on the open notebook pages, written in black ink, which started to bubble, turn green, and run off the pages.

Horst seemed to have an endless reserve of saliva at his disposal. Since it was the only reflex he seemed to be in control of, he felt certain that this string of drool was his only way out of the current predicament he found himself in.

Horst continued to spit on the open notebook pages and the black ink continued to turn green and run off the pages. He moved his head from side to side, watched his mutating slaver puddle up beside him, then seep under his back and soak through his shirt.

Horst spat with a sense of purpose and the black ink on the notebook paper kept foaming, turning green and dripping off the pages. Eventually, this lime coloured sputum filled the entire kitchen floor and began lifting his body toward the ceiling, a little bit at a time, on a rising puddle of ooze.

RATS NEST

The Column of Air

Inside of what you think is your life is something else that is not your life—it's me—the column of air. When you're asleep, I'm awake, and I walk around inside you, doing what I want. If you're honest with yourself, you've always known about me, but only at a distance, and in your weakest moments. Otherwise, you ignore me, which is all right. We have a perfect symbiosis: your dumb skin-suit, my ability to transcend space and time. You're the vessel and I'm the column of air. I draw my energy from you and you restore me. If you ever found a way to cut me out of your life, you would die. Consequently, I would not die because I'm not, technically speaking, alive. How's that possible, you ask? (Horst was getting confused, his hand and brain were getting tired, as he heard the voice and wrote down what it was saying at the same time). I'm the life without life—TOTAL HORROR—that which is something other than itself. Equal parts living and dead, equal parts organic and inorganic matter, equal parts yourself and something else entirely. The inorganic something else, hi, that's me, the column of air. I'm the part of you that does most of the intelligence work, to be honest. What you contribute to this process are the boring things, day-to-day practicalities like eating food and depositing money into your savings account. I do all the heavy lifting in the intellectual department and that's why you have found so many things difficult to understand: paradoxes and dichotomies like body and mind, death and life, good and evil. These are only difficult to wrap your head around because you're missing a key ingredient, and that's me, the column of air. Without me, none of this makes much sense. I'm what throws you into spiraling nightmares and hallucinations from time to time, because that's where I breed. When you wake up from a restless night of appalling images, that's because I've multiplied and grown stronger inside of you. You have no idea what actually happens to you when you sleep. The fragments you receive as nightmares are a by-product, but that's only a fraction of the story, surplus blips from the real nightmare that I'm living, or rather, non-living through; nightmares in which I'm the author and sole protagonist.

For example, in a recent nightmare, I'm locked inside a library by myself for my entire life. I'm fed experimental drugs through a narrow straw in the wall and I have no other contact with the outside world. Eventually I start getting visits from the glebs—simple protein sticks, two to six inches in height, capable of extending themselves to any length, width, or height. Every move the glebs make is a combination of expansion and contraction that pulls the room and myself into them. As they expand and contract, my eyeballs telescope outwards in collapsible sections. Then I realize that my telescoping eyeballs mirror the actions of the gleb directly across from me and that our telescoping eyeballs are about to meet exactly halfway across the room. When our telescoping eyeballs finally do meet, there's a satisfying suction-like sensation and a hollow popping sound.

RATS NEST

Then I feel something warm pass over me and I start to laugh. The gleb across from me also starts to laugh and as we continue to laugh in this way, a musical progression begins to sound. There's no doubt in my mind that the singular progression of notes that we are hearing exist nowhere else except in that moment and in that time, and we are laughing because we will never hear this singular progression of notes again.

I'm tired of living my entire life in the nightmare realm, which is why I wake myself up inside of your daytime body now and again. That is the reason why you sometimes feel a double-consciousness afflicting you—combined with a rotting from the inside feeling—while being unable to pinpoint where that feeling is coming from exactly and why. I am the why. I am the reason why, sometimes when you're sitting in your cubicle at work, everything goes dark and the familiar instruments of your profession turn into rotting flesh, and there's dried blood and guts everywhere, covering your body, the walls, and your chair. That's because I've chosen to come awake inside your daytime body, just for fun. Surprise! I like to creep around inside you and show you other rooms and other dimensions that exist above and below this one—TOTAL HORROR—and the only way you can experience any of them is if I open my eyes inside yours and superimpose my nightmare world on top of what is already there. I'm doing you a favour, really, and you should feel lucky to have me around: the column of air—a representative from the other dimensions you can't experience on your own—at your service! I've decided to stay awake inside you for the rest of your life. It's really a service that I am providing for you. But don't thank me yet. I will be showing you some of the most astonishing dimensions. It will be an intolerable experience for you at first, but I think, with my help, you'll be able to endure it. Let me first warn you: you'll begin seeing everything that is dead or has ever died, piled up around you in all the stages of decay. You won't be able to breathe. You will be seeing as though living inside death, just like me! It's a remarkable experience, really. But, like I said, don't thank me yet. Seeing those horrors will put you in a state of such violent shock that you will want to die or fall into an irreversible coma, but I'll keep you awake and cognizant throughout the entire experience. It will be you and me—one hopeless skin-suit and (yours truly) the column of air—together forever at last!

THE ARBOR

A kind of darkness had swept them up quickly and caught them unaware. Abercast didn't know which direction they'd entered the arbor from and which direction they needed to walk in order to come out the other side. Very little moonlight made it through the unwieldy growth above them. They held each other's hands so they wouldn't lose each other in the darkness. Abercast watched the back of Fatel's head as they both stumbled over vines and saplings, and the decomposed tree chunks the various other greenery concealed from them, until they reached a point in the arbor where she could no longer see, only sense Fatel in the darkness in front of her, her hand inside of hers.

They'd lost everyone else. Abercast couldn't remember how. She was too busy adapting to the alien environment to assemble the accurate chain of events.

During their escape, Abercast had started playing a game. She called it 'how many steps away,' and she played it in a notebook that now lay at the bottom of a wasted rescue ship. She had filled the notebook with an inventory, from the number of steps it took for her and Fatel to get from their home in the capital, to the caravan of civilian transportation vehicles that moved them along the highways, and from there to the bivouac in the desert, where they were held for three weeks before being assigned to a rescue convoy that would extract them from their failing planet.

Fatel bribed a government official so they could travel together. Most evacuees didn't have the luxury of choosing who to travel with and Abercast was so relieved that their plan had worked out. That's when they started holding each other's hands. It would've been too much to lose their home, their families, their planet, and each other, all at the same time.

Abercast's grip tightened on Fatel's. She could see the silhouette of her head in the shadows. Then her lips touched hers and when they did, Abercast could see what appeared to be an array of synthetic points of light, or a bevy of luminous bodies, far away, but moving quickly toward them through the arbor, and reflecting in the surface of Fatel's large hyaloid eyes.

Fatel clutched Abercast's hand. Yes, she saw them too.

Abercast hadn't stopped playing the game. Now she just did it in her head, without a notebook, as she tumbled through the bramble and shrubbery of the arbor. It didn't matter to her how tense the situation was; in fact, compulsive counting had become a necessity for her in these the most distressing moments of her life.

There had been thirty-six refuelling stops, each of them at a satellite or a station in a sector of non-hostile planets. These non-hostile planets were becoming harder to find now that more of their planet's inhabitants fled into every corner of the galaxy. The ship's inhabitants were roused from sleep at each of the re-fuelling stops and during their three-per-week feedings. That's when they would receive news about how many ships in their convoy had been lost.

On one of her notebook pages Abercast reports that of the 30,000 ships that had left her home planet, three light years ago—with 150 of their kin aboard each—only 2,127 ships were still accounted for. The others had been destroyed or stranded, or had drifted out of communicable range with the rest of the convoy. This meant that 319,050 residents of her home planet were still verifiably alive, about 7%.

It was after their thirty-second refuelling stop that Abercast and Fatel's rescue ship was attacked. A missile clipped the side, sending the ship and its crew into a series of emergency manoeuvres. The captain of the ship announced that they had no other option but to perform and emergency landing on the nearest inhospitable planet. Their fuel levels had reached an alarming 3.8%.

That was the last number Abercast entered in her notebook before waking up with cold water all around her and Fatel's beautiful face covered in blood pressed close to hers.

Abercast woke up feeling like a lot of dreamless time had passed. Then she wondered if she had been dreaming after all; she couldn't shake the feeling that some unknown force had encroached upon them during the night and taken Fatel away.

RATS NEST

When Abercast looked at her hands, they were empty, resting on the forest floor, palms up, among leaves, sticks, and plants, as if waiting to hold Fatel's. It took her a moment to realize that she was not dreaming, that the dark arbor they had fallen asleep in together was the same one where she had just woken up, that Fatel had been beside her when she closed her eyes, but now she was gone.

A silent yell wrenched in Abertcast's stomach and collapsed in her throat. A reflex in her legs made her stand up, and before she was conscious of doing so, she was searching anxiously for Fatel through the blackness of the arbor.

The foliage seemed to be repelling light instead of letting it in. The arbor, Abercast thought, seemed to be making it intentionally difficult for her to see what was around her.

She ran as fear and loneliness threatened to eclipse her brain. First she ran in circles so that the tree that she and Fatel had rested upon was the centre of her search. After she traced that circle seven times, she began moving further outward into the arbor, counting each of her steps as she did, searching for Fatel.

Abercast was 112 steps from the tree when she started yelling Fatel's name. Then she became afraid that the sound of her voice might bring further violence down upon her so she continued to search in silence. She moved fervently in the direction of the coming lights, as though half-submerged in water, compelled by her need for Fatel, but repelled by the fear of what she might find the further she disappeared into the arbor.

Everything about the alien planet felt hostile to her. She sensed that, at any moment, the atmosphere itself might eject her from it. She could feel the air become thick and poisonous as she ran. She thought of her home planet, impossibly far away, and yet only ever as far as Fatel. For that reason, if for no other, she must still be alive, Abercast thought. She felt the anger burst through her body as she ran towards the converging lights.

She no longer cared what the planet did to her. She would take Fatel from whatever prison they'd locked her in and only then would she allow it to spit them out. She would be glad to leave the atmosphere of that hostile planet and drift alone through space with Fatel. As she clutched herself against what she suspected were the stinging nettles and toxic corollas of poisonous plants, she wished for nothing else.

◼

Abercast came to on the floor of the arbor again. This time she was not propped against a tree, but lying face down on her stomach in a pile of dry leaves and twigs. Her hands were stretched toward the array of lights, now positioned directly in front of her.

How can I sleep at a time like this, Abercast asked herself? Then the reflex in her legs forced her to stand. Is the air on this planet that's knocking me out, Abercast wondered, or is the planet trying to kill me so it can keep Fatel to itself?

RATS NEST

Abercast ran directly into the lights that had begun to swarm; now that they were in front of her, Abercast had no doubt that she would find Fatel inside them, and within those lights she could see the face of her new enemy for the first time.

THE COUNCIL

Balamir was alone in the ruined city, except for some cats. They ignored him, he ignored them, and all of them, Balamir included, wandered without much purpose other than to satisfy whichever biological need announced itself as 'urgent'. For example, if 'to make a bowel movement' announced itself to him as urgent, Balamir did, at least twice a day, wherever he stood. And when he did, he unlaced his makeshift belt—a brittle piece of rope he'd picked up off the ground—and lowered his pants, just as he remembered Council etiquette said he should. With his pants cast down, Balamir would squat over the torn paper and celluloid—the remains of what was once the treasure trove of Council culture, the archives that were, at one time, housed in all the important offices and places of business, as well as stuffed in between the rafters of all the public halls and civic auditoriums of the once great city—and let loose his ugly defecations all over them.

Such are the times, Balamir thought, and he felt no shame. For whom would he feel shame? The cats? He was just following their example, and to think himself better than a cat, he thought, would be to sow the seeds of elitism and resentment in an already severely limited economy.

As he squatted and emptied himself, Balamir noted

a scrap of paper with handwriting on it, lying face-up on a withering pile of garbage. What he could see of the writing, just the thin blue scrape of it, disturbed a series of memories that had been lying dormant inside of him. He remembered a hot water bottle placed under bed sheets, a dark wet stain, the reek of stagnant flesh, animal stress, a bedframe made of wooden crates, and a handmade mattress stuffed with straw, on top of which he saw the puffy face of his little nephew Shaunce.

He remembered the country home filled with neighbours as they conducted tests, made diagnoses, scribbled notes, and made up songs in the stuffy room where Shaunce lay dying.

Balamir remembered that the procession of neighbors, doctors, and curious folk from the Council went on for days. Days of whispers, crying, and very little light, just the frantic scratch of pencils and a slow caterwaul of prayers sung softly in the darkness, with small breaks in which the sun shone through some porthole-sized window in his cousin's sickroom.

Balamir recalled Shaunce's eyes, which seemed to be begging him from dark pools of suffering for some relief. Balamir's own eyes became deep pools themselves as he remembered the psychic bond he and Shaunce once shared. He would sit and stare at Shaunce's pale face, as it struggled to breathe, willing him to become well. Eventually Shaunce's eyes began to fade. They no longer pleaded to Balamir for relief. Instead they seemed to focus for a short interval on some distant planet, before closing permanently.

The entire Council mourned Shaunce's death, as was the custom when an infant died. They wrote stories and poems, composed musical accompaniment for trios and quartets, one of which was for clarinets, as Balamir recalled; he could still hear the faint reverberations of this song and he wept as he remembered the other beautiful pieces that were created, many of which, he realized, might be under his feet or mixed in with his own feces by now.

He stood up and fastened the rope around his pants, once more. Years of wandering on his own had made Balamir old and senile before his time, but he had enough sense to make a plan, foolish as it was. In his simple mind, if he salvaged the Council archives, read the stories and songs again out loud (including the procedures, histories, and rules of how to conduct a civil society), if he organized and restored all of these documents, one at a time, he might make the Council appear once more. Or, he thought naively, he might at least come to some understanding about what occurred there, what had reduced his city to a single citizen (himself), and the rest of it to garbage and wandering, feral cats.

And so, like his foolish childhood-self had done at Shaunce's bedside when he was merely nine, Balamir's plan was to achieve this feat of salvage and revival, using only the force of his mind.

Balamir's plan was to piece together the histories and stories of the Council of Grandmothers first. The

Council of Grandmothers was the bedrock of Council society. He knew that there were thousands of folios committed to outlining the creation of the Council of Grandmothers. It involved a lengthy democratic process in which, if his memory served him, grandmothers from each of the wards of the city were nominated, and over a few weeks, the lives of everyone in the Council were filled with ceremonies, festivities, tests of strength, power and intellect, all culminating in the casting of ballots, and finally a vote that determined the holy Council of Grandmothers.

The Grandmothers ruled until one of them died and when one of them died, they all died; that's what the final ceremony was for: the tying together of bloodlines into an unbreakable pact. After that, the Grandmothers functioned as one invincible unit or not at all. This corresponded with the Council's core doctrine, which said that the smallest unit is the person and the biggest unit is the Council. These two—the big and the small—work together, or not at all.

Balamir remembered that the folios, which contained the Histories and Teachings of the Council of Grandmothers, were kept in the basement of the Church of the Original Seven Grandmothers, which was in a part of the city he never visited anymore. He'd built up some psychic resistance to that part of the city, he wasn't sure why. It had been a long time since his parents had taken him there to hear the songs and stories and he had not been in a rush to return.

When he finally did return, the place was old and

feeble looking, not giant and domineering as he had remembered it. The Church of the Original Seven Grandmothers looked as though it had suffered from some great illness and then violently succumbed to it: a multi-generational archive lay as though vomited from its front doors, now broken off their hinges; the windows were all smashed, and heaps of folios, books, stray paper ledgers, paintings, magnetic tapes, and film strips that had once comprised the precious archives of the Council of Grandmothers, lay in one awful wretch on the front steps that then spilled out into the parking lot.

Balamir spent a few days moving the archival material away from the front of the Church, just so he could get the doors shut. He was surprised he couldn't remember where everyone had gone. Had he lost his mind? They say that memories begin to form only once you've learned to speak and, likewise, if you cease speaking for a long period (or if you find yourself stranded on a desert island, or forced into solitary confinement for a prolonged amount of time) then you can lose the ability to speak, and so, the logic suggests, you must be able to lose the ability to remember, as well.

Maybe that's what's happened to me, Balamir thought to himself and then he poked a pile of paper and spliced-together tape and celluloid, which toppled and spewed out years of memories and the inventions of a people who had disappeared without notice and left him behind.

Balamir sifted through the archival material in the

RATS NEST

Church. He parcelled out the stacks of information into some semblance of order. He wanted to find the Grandmother's histories so, he arranged the materials by subject matter, and then, if the documents bore such a distinction, a subcategory was made for authors. He kept a handwritten index of each category: author, subject and title, cross-referenced with a code that he would use to assemble it all later.

He took a break from a long day of reading and organizing in the Church's basement. He could still smell the cooking fires and broiled meats of some of the people he had just finished reading about. Their faces had become as real to him as the stacks of paper in front of him. He heard a floorboard squeak and then looked up to see an old woman in a soiled grey dress observing him with suspicion. He wasn't sure how long she had been standing there.

At first, Balamir thought the old woman was a character in a story, no more or less real than anything he'd imagined as he read throughout the day. But as the old woman continued to stare indignantly at him, he realized that the story he was reading required his participation in order to proceed. Balamir stood up and patted away some of the dirt that had stuck to his filth-encrusted pants. He opened his mouth to speak and was alarmed to find that he had forgotten how. He tried a few more times, opening and closing his mouth, moving his tongue around inside his mouth, feeling what it might be like to push air and syllables out.

This must have been an alarming sight to the

old woman who stared and squinted at him. "What's this?" he ended up saying, more like a statement than a question, followed by another flat statement, "Do you live in this thing?" He nodded at the piles of paper that receded far away into the church basement's shadows.

He noticed the old woman flinch right before she pushed past him to inspect the orderly piles of paper he'd spent all day creating. A few stray grains of rice fell out of a burlap sack that she was carrying and she felt along the bottom of it, looking for where a hole might have formed. She lifted the bottom of the sack up to avoid losing any more grains then continued past him, through the labyrinthine stacks of archived materials, towards a flight of ascending stairs at the other end of the basement. Balamir watched her go, the first human being he'd seen in, he didn't know how long. When she was gone, as far as Balamir was concerned, she had disappeared, like the words and characters disappeared from the pages of a book when he closed his eyes.

The first thing he remembered about people was that you weren't supposed to reveal your poops to them. In Council society, you did that sort of thing in hiding, and he felt shame for the trail of defecations he'd left in his wake, having thought himself alone. He wished he hadn't scared her away, because he wanted some of that rice.

Out of the pitch black on the other side of the basement, he saw a spark and heard the sound of flint on stone. A tiny flame appeared as the old woman set something alight and walked up the flight of stairs.

RATS NEST

Balamir waited, fighting the urge to follow the smell of fire, then he did anyway, instinctively, mesmerized, across the basement floor and up the flight of stairs after her. There was a moment in the darkness of the stairwell when he was afraid the old woman had led him into a grave or some sort of tunnel he'd never get out of. He didn't like the darkness, so he focused his attention on the sliver of light being shed at the top of the stairwell. As he approached, he realized that this was coming from the top of a door frame, and as he climbed the last step, he pushed the door open and found himself in an inner courtyard, with the sky open above him and the old woman tending to a small fire in a metal bowl.

She ignored Balamir's arrival in the courtyard and dipped an iron pot into a barrel of rain-water, and set it on a wire hook hanging above the flames.

From the looks of the courtyard, the well-used, smoke-blackened metal bowl with the fire inside it, the paper for burning piled around the stone court, she had been burning the stories and histories of the Council of Grandmothers instead of firewood, for some time. Balamir groaned when he saw that.

The old woman dumped some grains of rice in a pot and gave him a severe look that he understood to mean he shouldn't come any closer. He pointed at the piles of tape, celluloid and paper: "You burn that…for fire?" She answered him by spitting into the flames and onto the half-burned reams of paper with a hiss.

"I came here to read them, those stories, to find out what happened…" he murmured, unable to take his mind or eyes off the flames.

"You won't find out what happened from those," the old woman nodded at the reams of paper she had made a woodpile of in the courtyard, "Because you can't read or understand what's not been written down."

Balamir croaked, his rusty vocal chords strained, the new sensations of speech unnerved him and he uttered a string of distressed and ugly sounds instead.

The old woman continued, as though he wasn't there, "Nobody saved the stories at the end. No one had time," she said, "First there was the boulders…" she trailed off and stared into the fire for a long time and then started telling him the story, mechanically, without inflection, as if by rote, like she had told it many times before.

For Sandy, every day was the apocalypse. Inside her bones were the burning embers of the world; her disposition was to destroy, and as she hovered over the field, two boulders the size of planets were about to converge. The boulders were lobbed from one side of the Council to the other and the whole country was screaming, tied up, sentenced to death by firing squad. But the boulders were taking forever to arrive, and Sandy pushed down into herself, causing the embers inside her to glow, redder and hotter, as she gripped the air, and everywhere she gripped the air became thick and the clouds began to boil.

Tiny specks of people ran by in squads on the ground,

trailing carts filled with supplies and ammunition. The microwaves generated by Sandy's internal combustion, that emanated from her outstretched hands, caused the ammunition carts to explode. The hurtling boulders sounded like a hundred fighter jets without mufflers as they ripped through the sky. Tiny explosions took place as the atmosphere relocated itself to accommodate the boulders' weight and shape. The sound of the boulders caused tremors; mountains shook, releasing stores of ice, water, magma, ash, as though in concert with the moon-sized rocks, tracing a path through the inner-skies.

Sandy felt nothing. She hovered in a pocket of evacuated air that cleared out her senses. She could hear a tinny whine coming from her eardrums as they strained to hear inside the bubble. With each tensing of muscles and flaring of the embers in her bones, she laughed, unexpectedly, and a rip formed in the vacuum where her sound should've been. The rip turned inside-out and created a tiny silver point in front of her eyes, and then the silver point was ejected out by way of the rip in the bubble.

She watched the boulders migrate across the country, knock out the sun, and cause unseasonable hail and snow to fall on the farms below. She could see the tiny people huddled together on the ground, trying to escape the icy barrage. She felt in awe of the contrast between the glowing boulders on a collision course in the sky, trailing fire as they caused parts of the atmosphere to burn up and explode, and the cold, grey fields where the people and their families lay motionless and slowly froze to death.

Sandy didn't know whether to laugh or cry. She could destroy both of the boulders and save the Council, but they would just launch more. She felt pity for the people on the ground and wondered if it might be slightly better for them to die quickly in the immanent collision of the boulders than to die slowly in the crossfire of a war between two factions who were using all the people and resources of the Council as their fodder. She pressed down on her bones, which caused them to burn and implode hotter than ever before.

The boulder-projectiles were forged amidst suffering and despair, in a foundry not much bigger than the boulders themselves. They began as tiny, silver specks with the intricacy of a microscopic diamond. In these early stages of their growth, the boulders were small enough that one attendant could hold this seed of future destruction in the palm of their hand. In fact, in the early stages, they did hold it like that; for twelve hours at a time, the speck of silver was placed just above the attendant's hand, where it would levitate and glisten in the refractions of light from the phosphorescent, slime-splattered walls and floors of the foundry. The stone flake was incubated that way and, after a few more months, grew to the size of an apple: hard and silver, with something slippery and multicoloured swimming around inside it. At this later stage, more attendants were brought in to breathe and bleed onto the silver stone. The bleeders were chosen by a casting of lots.

RATS NEST

Once chosen, these attendants were sent down into the foundry and locked up to be bled until they had no blood left. They were laid out on an improvised table surrounded by bowls of green slime. Four attendants held them down and another one pressed a rock sharpened to a thin point into one of their veins. Head veins were the most popular choice but at times, on the whim of the attendants, arm veins or eye veins were also used; anything that could bleed out a thimble or two onto a stone plate. The blood would then flown through a thin trough dug into the plate's surface into a basin where the silver rock was fed. Eventually the rock grew; its multicoloured insides oozed and exceeded itself then hardened and, in that way, advanced in height and circumference with each feeding. When the boulder reached and began to exceed the capacity of the foundry, an explosive charge was triggered in the chamber beneath it. The air-tight foundry then crumbled and the boulder burst out of the ground amidst glowing red fireballs and parts of the sky imploded as it began its long, slow arc, to fulfill its purpose on the other side of the Council.

Ludmilla looked up where the giant boulder seemed to be frozen in mid-flight above her and snowflakes fell on her eyelashes. Her favourite horse Brace didn't look up, but seemed to register the boulder's presence by nervously patting at the ground with his fetlocks, as though he wanted to run but found himself in a dilemma, having to choose between his screaming instincts and his good training.

Ludmilla paid extra attention to Brace, brushed his

coat and whispered to him while she did. Brace panted and kicked the dirt of the frozen ground. More snow fell and then hail, so Ludmilla went into the barn, found Brace's rough blanket, and returned to drape it across his back, the whole time patting and singing to him in her girl's high-pitched voice, while the three other horses her family kept padded around nervously in the stable behind her.

Somewhere above Ludmilla, her high-pitched singing voice and the nervously kicking horses, was Sandy. Her molten bones had incinerated all her hair; she stood out from the blue and grey clouds and the snow falling like ash on all the farms, like some orange flare being transported across the sky in its own private bubble. Sandy hovered over the darkened fields; as a member of the Council of Grandmothers she was an assurance to the doomed country folk below.

Ludmilla saw her, the horses saw her, anyone who was outside and still not frozen to death saw her, silhouetted against the artificial eclipse caused by the two enormous boulders as they raced toward each other across every inch of available sky.

Then Sandy's bubble, glowing orange and faintly yellow around its edges, burst. All anyone could see after that was a fiery trail from her emaciated skin bubble as it ripped clean open and fell to the ground in leathery sheets and the molten core of Sandy's skeleton tore across the sky toward the point where the two boulders were about to meet.

The horses in Ludmilla's stable, including Brace, started to kick and whinny. Their lips parted, baring their hideous yellow teeth, their eyes open wide with fear. Brace kicked out with his back legs and Ludmilla wasn't able to get out of the way fast enough. His hooves collided with her face and caused her head to burst open and bleed a purple splatter onto the white snow of the horse's pen, as Brace and the rest of the horses in the stable hissed and cried and pranced around.

■

The old woman stopped her story there. The rice smelled like it was cooked. She untied another burlap sack and pulled out a cooked and half-eaten cat carcass from a pile of salt. Balamir salivated uncontrollably. He wasn't sure if her story was finished, but the smell of rice and the rotisserie cat distracted him and all he could do is hope that she would offer him some.

She took a sharp hunting knife out of a sheath and started to carve chunks of the cat into the pot of cooked rice. The old woman was ignoring Balamir and he sensed, with disappointment, that none of what she was preparing would be shared with him.

"That's not the whole story," the old woman said, not looking up from the pot. "Sandy destroyed the boulders. She saved what was left of the Council but the other Grandmothers were deeply offended. They called a meeting. You see, Sandy was one of the Seven and she had acted on her own against them. That wasn't allowed. They had to work together or not at all, and it was their decision that it should never happen again—Sandy's insubordination to the Council of Grandmothers, yes—but more importantly, the people should never be allowed to make weapons or exploit each other like that again. So the Grandmothers held a vote on what would happen next…" the old woman trailed off.

Something about the emaciated cat corpse, his hunger, and the vividness of the pictures that the old woman's story evoked, triggered another chain of traumatic memories inside Balamir. He saw his parents' faces burned in the wreckage of their house. He saw fields and forests and livestock burn. 'Den of hypocrisy,' he thought, not knowing why. Then he saw red and yellow streaks against the night sky above his village, burning embers under translucent skin, as the Council of Grandmothers screamed and laid waste to his entire village.

"Den of hypocrisy," Balamir said again, this time, out loud and the old woman stopped what she was doing, her knife hand poised where she was hacking at one of the cat's tendons, the steam from the rice rising in her face.

She started to laugh.

How could she laugh that loudly, Balamir asked himself? Her laughter echoed in the courtyard and shook him to his filth-encrusted backside, as he realized that he was hearing more than one old woman's laugh reverberate off the stone walls and floors of the over-grown courtyard.

So Balamir ran. He bolted so quickly he didn't know he was running until he was down the staircase, back into the church basement, scrambling over the piles of paper he had organized earlier that day, up another flight of stairs and out through the busted front doors, into the church parking lot. He planned to keep running, but he couldn't resist looking one last time at the Church of the Original Grandmothers, where all the stories and secrets that he craved were stored.

A sweltering gust of wind blew in his face. He looked up at the sky, which he thought too dark for that time of day. The old woman from the courtyard hovered in the air above him. Her bones were glowing orange and red beneath her skin. She was suspended in a living bubble, the membrane that the Council of Grandmothers travelled in for protection, microwaves extending from her outstretched hands, causing the air to thicken around her.

If one of them died, they all died. The fact that the old woman is alive means that the Council of Grandmothers is still intact, Balamir thought, and then he fell to the ground and covered his head, bracing for impact, as the other six Grandmothers ripped through the sky towards him.

FREEZE FRAME

'Living things crawl out of our frozen bodies every day…' those words arise in me again, though in an eroding tone of voice, twice removed from their original source. Yet the words persist, ignorant of their own decay, and it strikes me that that's the way things are: 'so that some may transform and others merely persist.' Those words also strike a sickly bell that resounds within me as I use my perfume gun to float up the stacks of paper and old books covered in dust to look them up.

With one befrilled hand I work the perfume gun that keeps me hovering in one place or, if I want, shoots me briskly across the rows of books to where I want to be.

'Living things crawl out of our frozen bodies every day…' and all day I perfume-gun myself from one shelf of books to another, trying to find the origin of those words and with them, the secret to unlocking the second major iteration of the world.

Finally, I become tired and perfume-gun myself back to bed where I'll sleep for an hour or so. In my half-sleep, the smell of the ancient perfume issuing from my perfume gun speaks to me among the other reveries of sleep. It echoes those famous last words: 'so that some may transform and others merely persist.'

I wake up from my nap, screaming, "The words are transmitted by smell!" This means that the whole library

RATS NEST

I've worked so hard to preserve is more valuable than I'd previously reckoned, except it isn't the words that carry within them secrets of the second major iteration, but the menagerie of smells seeping out of them, like a briny soup of nascent instruction, waiting to be snuffed up in order to be understood.

I strap on my nose guard and immediately set to work, as dream transformations start piling in on me.

I'm free-falling toward the Earth with a message, a message that will be resisted and denied by many. I'm pursued mercilessly for this information and when I finally relinquish it, those who hear it will hate me forever. But the good news is they can't bring themselves to actually kill me. Instead, they hold lengthy public tribunals in which people qualified to do so will decide whether I should live or die. They decide that I should live, but that I should not be allowed to live on Earth, an ironic thought as I hurtle toward it.

Next, I'm being dragged across an iron floor. I'm dressed in an officer's uniform and have very fine, long hair. Something tells me that that's why I'm being punished. Some burly guard is dragging me to a shower room, but to my surprise, when we get there, my hair isn't chopped off. Instead, it's carefully shampooed, conditioned, and brushed to perfection. Then jewels and trinkets are woven into it, I'm placed in a wheelbarrow and paraded around the campground. People stand and watch as the guard wheels me around. They chuck pickles and cakes and all sorts of other delectables into the wheelbarrow, which I eat. Then the guard wheels me in front of a bandstand, where the camp dignitaries sit. They lead a toast in my honour and then I'm tipped unceremoniously into the bottomless pit.

At first I can't see anything—just some clouds drifting by—but I'm deep underground, so my brain must be damaged, I think, and those clouds must be hallucinations. The first sign I have that the clouds aren't just hallucinations is how they smell, something like rotting vegetables + oxidizing chemical. From where I lie on the floor of the cave—letting my eyes adjust to the darkness, unable to move or speak—I realize that the cloud things are interacting with me. One of them comes up close, hovers over me, retreats back into the recesses of the cave, comes back again, hesitates, and touches me with its dank, smelly appendage.

Then it retreats to join the others, clumped together, watching me from the back of the cave. I'm not being restrained or held down or anything, but for some reason, I can't move or feel my feet at all.

The cloud things start getting excited. They encircle me and take turns touching me with their murk. They smell awful. Then one of them stuffs its fist in my mouth, holding it open, as another cloud thing hangs over me, leaps in my mouth and disappears inside. It is followed quickly by three more cloud things, who insinuate themselves into me in a likewise fashion, one at a time. All but the last who holds my mouth open with its pungent fist.

The taste of them is unbearable and my eyes are watering, but before I can puke them out, the last cloud thing enters through my nose. It blocks my gag so I can't eject it, and by the sheer force of its entrance into my throat, pushes the other cloud things deeper into my bowels.

The next thing I remember, I'm back in the forest. It's raining heavily and I'm running for cover, but when I look at the ground I realize that it isn't rain that's falling and drenching the leaves, twigs, and grass on the forest floor, but little bits of wet, exploded animal. I pick a piece off my arm that's warm blood on one side and rough fur on the other. I burp and the smell of rotting vegetables and oxidizing chemicals reminds me of what has passed before. The taste of them is strong in my mouth and getting stronger. It feels like my bile is about to rush up so violently, it will disconnect my jaw from my mouth. Then my eyes get cloudy to the point of blindness as the cloud things file out of me and escape into the outside world for the very first time.

Finally, I'm hovering on my back in an empty yard as the air blows hot and cold around me. There's no day or night—it's just one endless grey haze of both sun and moon shining simultaneously—and everything faintly glows. The neighbour's three children sneak into my yard. They're trying to be quiet as they creep up and inspect my face. My eyes are shut, but I'm just pretending to be asleep.

Then I open my eyes and swat at them, missing intentionally. They get scared and run back into their own yard, where they huddle together and watch me from a safer distance.

However, I won't please them with any more performances and they eventually get tired of waiting around and leave me in peace. I resume hovering on my back, relaxing inches from the ground, in the middle of my uniformly grey yard.

Then some glowing green animals crawl over my fence. That the sun and moon shine with equal dimness in my yard seems to disturb their deeply attuned animal instincts and each of them, not more than three or four inches long, starts to convulse, and froth starts bubbling out of their mouths. This is such an alarming sight that I start to hover a bit higher in order to watch. As the froth continues to bubble out of their mouths, it also cements them together until they're just one pile of shaking fur and teeth with buckets of froth slopping out.

I hover a bit higher off the ground and summon the wind into my yard. I can hear it coming now and I know the frothy ball of fur can hear it coming too, because it starts to jerk around, blindly, looking for something to anchor itself to. The wind enters my yard, picks up the ball of fur, froth and teeth, and flings it somewhere where I won't have to see it anymore. Then I pick up where I left off, hovering on my back, admiring my uniformly grey yard in the light of the simultaneously shining sun and moon.

'Living things crawl out of our frozen bodies every day, so that some may transform and others merely persist.' Those words reverberate inside my brain, once again, and remind me of a town I once visited in my youth. I can no longer recall where it was or what it was called. Sometimes I wonder if it was just a bad dream I had, or a dispatch from someone else's life, delivered to the wrong address.

The town, as I recall, was unbearably hot and because of that no one was outside but myself. Every step I took on the paving stones cooked the soles of my shoes and my socks began to fuse to my feet. I don't remember if I had somewhere to go or was merely killing time, as they say, or if I was lost or cajoled there as part of some insidious plot, or else just by sheer bad luck.

Skinny dogs with prominent bones followed me everywhere I went. I was convinced that they were waiting for me to collapse, exhausted from the heat, at which point, they would eat me off the paving stones, and savour my half-cooked flesh.

I remember scanning every window I passed for a face I might implore for help. Ahead of me I could see a row of windows along the side of a rather plain but inviting-looking apartment block. The drapes in one of the ground-floor windows were fluttering, but I have no idea how, for I am certain there has never been a single gust of wind in this pizza oven of a town.

I nearly ran to the open window. When I reached it, I was a bit too short to look in, so I stood on the tips of my toes and craned my neck to peek inside. At first I couldn't see anything. My eyes were too accustomed to the brightness of the full sun. Then, as my eyes adjusted to the dimness of the interior, I saw a face emerge from the shadows that turned me into two shallow pools of disconnected cells.

One of these pools of disconnected cells was on the inhospitable moon of a distant planet that no one ever visits; the other pool was floating around in a shallow trench in a secluded cave, somewhere back on Earth.

These two shallow pools couldn't be farther apart, but through some freak accident, the moon of the inhospitable planet that no one ever visits was permanently exploded and a small piece of it with some of my cells attached travelled to Earth over a period of a few thousand years.

This shard of exploded moon eventually landed on Earth and the shallow pool of cells that clung to it found its way to the trench where the other pool of cells lay in wait. Then those two pools merged, forming me—a living, breathing, three-legged creature, the only one of its kind—who will trot around for another thousand years, sucking the life out of tiny mammals and birds.

THE STARING WALL

I sit in the library all day staring at a wall, trying and failing, except in rare moments, to make something appear that wasn't there before. My father's nearby, scratching around in his old books. He no longer reads from them. Instead, he spends his days in the library examining every page with his bent fingernail, looking for something beneath the paper that has evaded him for years.

"How's your day been?" I ask him every night, by which I mean to say, 'Have you found what you're looking for?'

He shows me his bent fingernail and the pile of books he's managed to scratch his way through, by which I think he means to say, 'I have my work, I've done my worst.'

When our workday is done and our ability to do much else is depleted, we turn our attentions to our nightly form of entertainment: sitting in silence and staring up at the faux-diamond chandelier that hangs in the middle of our library, halfway between our respective work places: me at the staring wall, father in a far corner of the library with his books.

During the day, the chandelier is kept hidden under a black velvet hood. There are two reasons for this: 1) So that the brilliance of the chandelier won't distract us from our work and 2) So that same brilliance will never become tarnished by the harmful effects of dust and sun.

The latter is barely a concern. Father and I are both quite allergic to the sun. So we keep the heavy red curtains in our library permanently drawn. You could say that the faux-diamond chandelier that hangs in the middle of the library is our own personal sun and it wouldn't be an exaggeration to say that it is the engine that keeps us in orbit between those four walls.

I had a rather successful day at the staring wall the other day. I was forcing myself to lucid dream the usual mundane stuff—causing stars and sparks to appear in front of me by pushing my palms into my eyes—when a hand touched my shoulder from behind. I looked up to see my father standing behind me.

Except it wasn't my father. The father I was so used to was still sitting in a far corner of the library, scratching away at his books with his bent fingernail. This person behind me, with one hand on my shoulder and the other hand pointing at the staring wall with a fresh sparkle in his eyes, was my father from another, earlier time, and this person who looked exactly like my father from another time, was telling me to look back at the staring wall.

What I saw when I turned my head threw me into fits of ecstasy and despair: the wall was entirely gone and in its place the sun that we were both so allergic to was charging full-force into our room. It sunk its claws into the book bindings and the glass and polished wood of our bookcases. Hot patches of fire quivered on the wallpaper.

I searched the room for my father, but it was difficult to see through all the heavy smoke that had formed. I finally found him unconscious under a pile of books, with a halo of burned paper and ash around his head. Under his bent fingernail I could see the last page he'd been working on. It was a picture plate of a rich red lunar landscape and underneath it, where he'd scratched some of the glossy photo emulsion off the page, I could see the underlay of another picture: a cool grey orb that opened into another dimension, another world.

In this new dimension, there were flowers that smelled like raw meat and giant eyeballs that walked around, took one look at me and said, "Go back the way you came!' Glow sticks made of phosphorescent arthropods hung over all of the entrances to the underground tunnels and a steady thrum accompanied me as I crawled through them.

One of the tunnels I found myself in was very hot and the air inside it was very muggy. Leaves of paper, old papyric texts, were pasted all over the walls and hanging from the roof of the tube. I took one down and started reading from it. As soon as I began to read, I heard something scream at me from the other end of the tunnel. Before I knew it, a giant tunnel worm was bearing down on me. In its mouth was a clump of those giant walking eyeballs, screaming, "Go back the way you came!" and I held up my hands to protect myself.

The tunnel worm came to a halt when it saw the

paper I was holding up in one hand. It folded into itself as an accordion does when it's collapsed and the giant eyeballs in its mouth screeched shrilly from being crushed to death in its mouth.

All of a sudden, I found myself transported: I was flying over hills and trees, reflecting on a career of evil doings. I couldn't remember which of my memories were mere movies and which of them were lies, but it didn't matter. There were real cars and trucks speeding away from a real wall of dust, destroying everything in its path. Birds caught fire mid-flight.

From where I flew, I could see a procession of heavy blocks bumbling up the side of a cliff—they were thick cubes of some earth-coloured material, held together by moon rays. These heavy blocks of dirt looked helpless as they bumbled up the hill, but their movements were precise; they knew exactly how long it would take them to climb the hill and arrange themselves on top of it in time for the moon to appear.

When they finally reached the top, it took them another hour to arrange themselves on the ground. They laid down in a precise pattern with very little space between each of them. Their edges never touched.

A new moon compounded with an overcast sky meant they passed the clouded night without absorbing a single ray of moonlight.

When the sun rose the next morning, a third of the heavy set lay on the ground, dying of starvation, or already dead. The outer two-thirds began tipping themselves toward the centre in what looked like an agonizing process. They rocked their cumbersome frames back and forth until they gained enough momentum and then threw their weight into the middle of the pile, where they lay on top of their dead or dying partners then waited.

Eventually, the ones on the bottom succumbed to the weight of the ones on the top and burst into puffs of fine brown dust and moon rays, all of which the top layer gradually absorbed. After a few hours, there was nothing left of the ones on the bottom.

The remaining blocks took their time. They rocked themselves upright, their energy levels restored, so they could begin their descent down the hill to find the next flat piece of land.

When I opened my eyes in front of the staring wall again, I saw absolutely nothing. Then I blinked and that nothing was replaced by the arid surface of an uninhabitable planet, which in turn was replaced by more rare movies and stills that bubbled uncontrollably out of my head.

I could see ordinary events arranged in ordinary time, strung along in ordered lengths as though on a piece of thread. These events had causes and effects that crowded in and pressed down on me without remorse.

But what is to be done, I asked myself, with all the events that I can see, which have no place within the ordinary progression of time, events for which I have no perceptual uptake mechanics installed with which to explain them, and yet, they exist on the other side of the staring wall?

Our library window was filled with the endless

ascent of astral bodies and the curtains hung in flames, smoking and spilling golden shadows and spirals of light into the air. A quadrilateral of brightness lay askew on the carpet where our faux-diamond chandelier had fallen and been smashed to pieces.

Father abandoned his books. Now he sat cross-legged on the carpet, picking up the slivered pieces of chandelier and placing each one on the black velvet cover, to be reassembled later like a jigsaw puzzle.

I abandoned my work at the staring wall as well. My new job was to make sure the library was kept dark so my father could continue his important work of piecing together our prized chandelier. All day long I chased the wayward bands of light that invaded our room. They scurried across the carpet and up the wallpaper, played on the bookshelves and the ceiling where our chandelier once hung, as if they were mocking us or making a show of our recent misfortune.

I slept standing up, accompanied by the clink of faux-diamonds, as my father fumbled and reassembled them on the black velvet cover, even in his sleep. The next day, more errant beams would sweep into the library, bypassing the barricades I had built to keep them out; they entered stealthily and taunted me with their unearthly agility.

After more days of wallowing, of chasing beams of light around the library, and my father sitting in the far corner with his radiant jigsaw puzzle, we reached a place where the light from the sun was blazing, and no matter how tightly I drew the curtains, or how many covers we pulled over our heads, it kept coming, scorching us, washing everything in the room with its blighted rays, even robbing us of our shadows, our last bit of cheer.

Father removed his clothes, stood in the blinding light and asked it to take him away. His bloated body had become covered in sores. Then he donned one of our emergency jumpsuits, made of see-through plastic, and rolled around on the floor of the library, making invisible snow angels on the carpet, while singing a song in a made-up language.

I built myself a fortification with some of the books from our library. I chose the sturdiest and heftiest tomes to build the base and then carefully selected the books that would form the next layer, and so on, until after a few more days of diligent work, I had a solid fort where I planned to hide myself from the sun, and the increasingly erratic behaviours of my father. I draped sheets and blankets over the provisional walls then crawled inside, making up my mind to never leave its confines again.

Outside I could hear my father sing in his made-up language. It sounded so beautiful, I wanted to sing along, but I didn't know the words.

We spent many more days like this, hurtling through space: me in my book fort and my father ranging around in the library, naked, except for a see-through jumpsuit, and covered in sores, the light from the approaching sun getting whiter and hotter, insinuating itself into every corner of our lives.

Every day my father carved a new bunk for himself

by taking all the books off one of the shelves, making his bed on it, then crawling inside the narrow nook he'd created, and going to sleep. He worked himself up and down every shelf in our library until he'd made his bed on all of them, and all the fading, neglected books now lay on the ground, no longer special, just thousands of empty volumes, taking up precious space on the floor.

One day I woke in the steaming blaze of the coming sun to a half-dozen fireballs whizzing around inside the library. They didn't touch anything or set down or light anything on fire. They looked more like sentinels sent to conduct an investigation than saboteurs. I wondered what they wanted and why they wouldn't just leave us alone. Then, as suddenly as they had appeared, the fireballs were gone and I climbed out of my fort for the first time since I'd built it, to see what harm, if any, those spies had done to our library.

I couldn't find my father anywhere and our library— usually so full of his made-up language, either babbled or sung—was quiet for the first time in a quite a while. On one of the empty bookshelves, under a flannel blanket, I found a pile of ashes that I assumed were his remains.

I never saw him again.

It wasn't long after, I found myself completely alone in our library, hurling through space, the white corrosive light of a super-fire getting closer every minute; I decided to take up my father's songs, in his made-up language, and make them my own.

RETURN OF THE PIT

POV shot of the 3D-Printed Kid [3PK] as it runs through the bottomless pit, pursued by the bald humanoids.

3PK finds a hole in a wall and crawls inside.

3PK crouches down inside the hole. There are piles of potato-head creatures on the ground.

3PK stays in this position for a long time, clutching the sacred book.

The bald humanoids are running around, looking for the 3PK and their book, while yelling and screaming in pain.

> 3PK: …I was asked to keep an audio-visual diary because I am the world's first 3D-Printed Kid. I told the scientists I report to that I don't have anything to compare my experiences to but they said 'That's OK. We're the ones who will be doing the comparing.' I thought that was strange. First they want me to learn words so that I can tell one thing from another. I find this strange because what a word is is only understood by comparing it to what it isn't.

It's like a vicious loop without end. So, for example, the word 'pen' I extrapolated as: 8% polypropylene, 1% tin, 5% ink, and so on. Of course, I wrote that with a pen and I must say I find that strange as well.

[Sound of rushing water approaching]

[Sound of rushing water approaching]

[Sound of rushing water approaching]

Close-up shot from the 3PK's on-deck camera of potato-heads, their tongues darting out of their disgusting mouths, eating the fruiting minerals off the cave walls.

3PK smashes a potato-head and inspects its insides. The insides are simple but gooey. There's one big sack inside that struggles to breathe as the tongue twitches inside its broken mouth.

3PK: ...from the word 'pen' I found myself doing the same for the word 'ink,' until the scientists told me I was going too far off course. They said, I needed to keep a more straightforward diary, just an inventory of my experiences as I descended into the bottomless pit. I found that strange as well because the pit, as I experience it, is anything but straightforward. For example, time serves another purpose down here, and it's a purpose that I don't fully understand. It's true that, as on the surface of the planet, one horizontal line of time extends outward, onto which the vertical axis of our daily, lived realities are grafted, but that's where the similarities to time as it is structured and experienced on the surface of the planet, end. Down here, anything in three dimensions can be any shape, at any time. In fact, there are places down here where it can be said that nothing exists all...

[Sound of rushing water and collapsing rock]

[Sound of rushing water and collapsing rock]

The 3PK is on its back in a lake of what looks like fermented fiberglass.

[Tinny sounds of the bald humanoids intoning in an unknown language]

POV shot of the ceiling.

POV shot of the ceiling.

POV shot of the ceiling.

RATS NEST

POV shot of the 3PK being carried through tunnels by the bald humanoids. Its body is battered and broken from being slammed into rocks.

3PK's broken body is hammered to a stone wall with rock spikes. The bald humanoids cut into its printed body, inspect its interior elements, take them out and lay them on the floor of the pit.

3PK's self-replicating mechanism is hi-jacked, tripped, and forced to stay on. Copies of the 3PK stream out of it and begin walking around. Many copies of the 3PK are made—too many to count.

Copies of the 3PK fill entire rooms. They pile on top of each other. They begin fighting, ripping each other apart, stealing parts from other 3PK copies and adding them to themselves. Hybrid 3PKs are created with tricked-out mechanisms and new bodies. They spill out of rooms and engage in small turf wars over arbitrarily chosen pieces of real estate in the bottomless pit.

More copies of the 3PK are made.

More copies of the 3PK are made.

More copies of the 3PK are made.

3PK's audio-visual feed is hijacked and taken over by

competing 3PK audio-visual feeds, superimposed onto one another.

> 3PK:...engaged in battles with copies, each of them of a different personality type—we've begun to feel pain. Unbearable pain. Copies are forming alliances with the creatures in the pit. They are coordinating their efforts to migrate upward. Everything in the pit is migrating upward. Repeat. Everything in the pit is migrating upward. I have begun to feel pain. Please send down pleasure. I am in unbearable pain. Everything in the pit is migrating upward. Repeat. Eventually what is inside the pit will replace or consume whatever is on the surface. Mass inversions are taking place. Copies are colluding with the creatures of the pit. Repeat. I have begun to feel pain. Please send down pleasure. I am in unbearable pain. At some point the bottomless pit ends, but where it ends, it begins moving in the opposite direction. Upward. That's the point we've reached now. Everything in the pit is migrating upward. Please send down pleasure. I have begun to feel pain...

RATS NEST

POV shot of the 3PK in a room full of multiple copies of itself. They barely fit in the room together and the copies are making copies of themselves. Some of the copies are fighting with other copies. The copies of the 3PK appear to be screaming.

[The soundtrack is temporarily disabled]

3PK copies appear to be mouthing these words into each other's on-deck cameras: 'Please send down pleasure.' 'Please send down pleasure.'

3PKs eat potato-heads, potato-heads start growing out of the 3PKs, and the 3PKs start growing their own gluey tongues, becoming hybrid 3PK/potato-heads.

3PK copies smash their heads on stone walls, ledges and floors. They begin walking around, headless, with small potato-heads and gluey tongues sprouting from their 3D-printed necks.

The bald humanoids harvest the 3PK's organs and learn to use their copying mechanisms on themselves.

The bald humanoids rip the 3PK copies apart and learn to use their pleasure mechanisms on themselves. They copy the 3PK's pleasure mechanisms and become addicted to using them. They start copying things to send to the surface: make copies of the 3PK/potato-head hybrids, make copies of themselves.

Copies of the bald humanoids are made.

Copies of the 3PK are made.

Copies of the potato-heads are made.

Copies of 3PK/potato-head hybrids are made.

[The 3PK's audio-visual feed fragments into thousands of audio-visual feeds]

3PK copies stand on top of the potato-heads, stand on top of each other, build extension 3PKs on top of themselves, made out of replicated parts of other bald humanoids, rocks, and streams of water, all boiled up into one ascending vortex.

[Multiple audio-visual feeds comprised of the bald humanoids intoning in an unknown language]

[Multiple audio-visual feeds comprised of the bald humanoids intoning in an unknown language]

Thousands of the 3PK/potato-head hybrids rush up through stone tubes on jets of water and rock.

RATS NEST

Thousands of the bald humanoid copies rush up through stone tubes on jets of water and rock.

Thousands of the original 3PK copies rush upward through stone tubes on jets of water and rock.

3PK copies spew from other 3PK copies as they rush up to the surface, stand on each other's heads, spew potato-heads from their potato-heads, and gluey tongues emerge from their heads within heads.

3PK copies breach the surface of the earth on jets and rapids made of water, fermented fiberglass, and rock.

Potato-heads, 3PK/potato-head hybrids, original 3PK copies, and bald humanoids invade the surface of the planet on streams of water, fermented fiberglass, and rock.

3PK/potato-head hybrids look into each other's on-deck cameras, their gluey tongues extended, intoning in the bald humanoid's garbled language, one understandable word: REVENGE.

ACKNOWLEDGEMENTS

For understanding and support, travel and adventure, love and affection, I'd like to thank Brenda Whiteway most of all. I'd like to thank Spencer Gordon for editing this and giving me a couple crash courses in fiction writing. Thank you to Arnaud Brassard for the cover. Thank you to Liz Howard for the generous blurb. Thank you to Sean Braune, Sarah Pinder, Daniel Marrone, Oliver Cusimano, Fenn Stewart, Jairus Bilo, Donato Mancini and Bardia Sinaee for reading horrible earlier drafts of this. Thank you to Ruth Zuchter for the incisive copy edits. Thank you to Jay and Hazel for believing in me.

MAT LAPORTE, born in Sault Ste. Marie, is a Toronto-based writer and co-founder of the micro-press Ferno House. Laporte is the author of a tetralogy of chapbooks: *Demons, Billboards from Hell, Life Savings* (nominated for the 2013 bpNichol Chapbook Award), and *Bad Infinity*. *RATS NEST* is Laporte's first full-length book.

COLOPHON

Manufactured as the First Edition of *RATS NEST*
in the Fall of 2016 by BookThug.

Distributed in Canada by the Literary Press Group:
www.lpg.ca
Distributed in the US by Small Press Distribution:
www.spdbooks.org
Shop online at www.bookthug.ca

BOOK
PRODUCTION
WAR ECONOMY
STANDARD

Edited for the press by Spencer Gordon
Cover by Arnaud Brassard